SECRET MISSION

When US Marshal Thaddeus Jenkins rode into town on a secret mission, he was mistaken for a train robber and badly beaten up. But he was determined to apprehend the real robbers, a particularly vicious bunch of killers. This was due to be Thaddeus's last mission and it looked as if he would not survive it. He had already taken a beating that would have killed most men, but nothing would stop him if only he could survive the bullets that were winging his way!

ZEKE MARTIN

SECRET MISSION

Complete and Unabridged

LINFORD
Leicester

First hardcover edition published in
Great Britain in 2003
Originally published in paperback
as 'Troubleshooter!' by V. Joseph Hanson

First Linford Edition
published 2004
by arrangement with
Robert Hale Limited
London

British Library CIP Data

Martin, Zeke
    Secret mission.—Large print ed.—
Linford western library
1. Western stories
2. Large type books
I. Title II. Hanson, Vic J. Troubleshooter!
823.9′14 [F]

ISBN 1–84395–380–3

Published by
F. A. Thorpe (Publishing)
Anstey, Leicestershire

Set by Words & Graphics Ltd.
Anstey, Leicestershire
Printed and bound in Great Britain by
T. J. International Ltd., Padstow, Cornwall

This book is printed on acid-free paper

1

He was a spindly, swarthy younker with lank, black hair. He entered the store with a swagger, his gun bobbing a little in the holster at his hip. His riding-boots were scuffed and he wobbled on them a little like any down-at-heel cowboy.

He passed over the shady, sun-speckled threshold and looked about him. There was a certain shiftiness in his eyes, which belied his pose of nonchalance. His face was a little sullen; his lower lip protruded a little like a naughty child's.

Two oldtimers sitting beside the pot-bellied stove looked him over then went on with their crack-voiced discourse.

Lye Mowbray, the tubby storekeeper, greeted him with a soft, 'Good-mornin', suh.'

The reply was flat, uncompromising. 'Mornin', I want some forty-five shells, some string baccy, a pair o'socks.'

'Yes, suh.' The storeman turned his head and called softly: 'Anna.'

A girl came out of the shadows behind the counter. The storeman said:

'Serve this gentleman, will you?'

'Yes, father.' She rested her hands on the counter-top and gave the young man an interrogative glance.

He repeated his order and smiled a little as he did so. It was an upward quirk of his lips which did not crinkle his face very much. It was the smile of a man who did not smile often. His eyes had taken on a new light, which had nothing to do with the smile, as he appraised the girl boldly.

She was very dark; her hair long, wavy and blue-black to her shoulders without ornament of any kind. Her eyes were large and brown, her lips full and richly red. Her face was perfectly modelled. As she turned away from him with a slight toss of her head he could see that her body, in shirtwaist and skirt, was well-built and shapely. Her movements were light and sure and there was a ripple of muscles where the shirtwaist was tight beneath her arms.

He watched her as she reached an arm up to the shelves. She held up a pack of tobacco. 'Will this brand do?'

'That'll do.'

She turned back to him with the baccy and a large box of shells. She pushed an open box in front of him and said, 'Choose your socks.'

He picked a dark pair at random, his eyes still on her most of the time, aggressively so, until finally she flushed a little and turned away. Then his eyes left her. He looked around.

'I'll have a few yards of that cloth,' he said, pointing to a roll of dark grey stuff.

'Ideal for patching,' she said. Her smile was a little strained.

'Yeh,' he said. 'I'll take six yards.'

She cut it off for him, put it with the other articles and made the whole lot up into a parcel. She did this deftly, unaware of his scrutiny now. She took the crumpled bill he tossed on the counter. As she gave him change their eyes met again.

'Thank you, miss,' he said and smiled once more. She was to remember that smile very well.

★ ★ ★

He crossed the narrow sun-baked street to where another man was standing with two horses by a hitching-rail. A stocky man with only one good eye, the other a mere red slit.

The younker said: 'Let's get a drink.'

The other said: 'The boss says to get what we want then move. No hangin' about — no drinkin'.'

'Aw, hell, Brodie, one ain't gonna do no harm. Yuh bin standin' at this hitching-rail here in front o' the saloon for the last few minutes lettin' everybody look at yuh — it's gonna look queer if we rode off now without goin' in for a drink.'

4

'Doggone it, Slim,' said Brodie. 'You got an argument f'r everythin'.'

'Come on,' said Slim. 'It ain't gonna take no more'n a coupla minutes. You'd like a drink, wouldn't yuh, Brodie?'

'Yeh, sure, but . . . '

Slim was already crossing the boardwalk. Brodie shrugged and followed. Above their heads a peeling sign which proclaimed that the establishment was *Kavanaugh's Bar* creaked a little in the dusty breeze. The dust was red and it laid a film over everything. It blew in from the Arizonian desert beyond, the beautiful, treacherous 'badlands' on the edge of which the town stood. There, too, just outside the town, at the foot of the craggy monstrosity known as 'The Devil's Fingers,' was the small mine which had brought sudden prosperity to the little place and caused a big Chicago financier to build a branch railroad line which ended there.

Men said that now, after six months, the gold was petering out, that the workers were discontented because they had to wait for wages, that the financier had not been able to cover his losses and was going bankrupt.

It was the main topic of conversation among the habitués of *Kavanaugh's Bar* that morning Slim and Brodie entered the place. The talk died a little and men turned and looked at them because they were strangers.

They ordered *tequila*, which nobody there drunk much any more — but they were not Mexicans. Sam Kavanaugh, who waited on bar himself of mornings, found half-a-bottle for them.

The young man, his glass in his hand, leaned against the bar and looked around him, but his eyes did not rest anywhere for long; they were perpetually moving, black berries in his sullen face. His companion had more of a hangdog look: he stared into his drink and took no notice of anybody. But many people noticed he had only one eye. They wondered if the two strangers were connected with the mine. If so, why did they not drink in their own cantina at the edge of town? They did not look like workmen, but just saddle-tramps. Then where were they heading? Jonestown led to no place; the nearest ranch was five miles away; the nearest big town was Nogales, where the railroad wound across the border. Maybe the strangers were prospectors. Gold had been found in the Devil's Fingers on the edge of the Sierra Madre: was it not possible that there was plenty more further on in the tortuous range of mountains. But whereas the narrow creek at Jonestown was adequate for panning the precious yellow stuff, lack of water anyplace else in the mountains made prospecting very unpractical — any tenderfoot should know that. And these men were not tenderfeet. Neither did they look like prospectors. They looked like trouble-shooters. Trouble-shooters were needed at the mine to swell the ranks of the guards who always rode with the goldtrain. If the strangers came for this purpose they must be made to understand, if they came in *Kavanaugh's Bar* again, that they were not wanted there and should drink in their own cantina.

The two men left the bar and eyes that watched them go noted they did not make for the mine, but went in the other direction, out on to the scrub which was the edge of the grasslands, the trail which led back to civilization. So the strangers were dismissed as saddle-tramps with ants in their pants and the people of Jonestown did not expect to ever see them again.

Slim and Brodie crossed the railroad tracks and rode down into a valley. On the opposite ridge, about two miles away, was a belt of woodland etched darkly against the skyline.

'Kale certainly picked his spot well,' said Slim. 'From up there he can see all the surrounding territory. I'll bet he's got his glasses on us right now.'

'Kale's smart,' said Brodie.

'Yeh, he's smart awlright.'

The two men waded their horses

across the creek which curved in deeply up ahead and ran behind the mine workings, and began to forge uphill gently again.

The wood became clearer and they could pick out the gnarled, sun-tortured shape of each individual tree on the edge of it. Suddenly a horseman rode out of the deeper shadows behind and came slowly towards them.

Man and horse were big. A black stallion and a man in black to match. A dark, hawk-featured man, almost a larger, older edition of the younker, Slim, but more untamed and cruel looking. Knowing it and glorying in the fact, wearing sombre clothes like a figure of doom.

'Howdy, Jack,' said Slim.

Jack Kale said: 'It's taken you long enough.'

Brodie said nothing and Slim chose to ignore the black-clad man's remark. He said: 'We got everything.'

Without another word Kale turned his horse and led the way back into the

9

trees. There, in a clearing were gathered a bunch of men, squatting on the ground in a circle while their horses cropped the short grass behind them.

The men greeted the two newcomers then went back to their card game. Slim, Brodie and Kale put their horses with the rest. Then the big man led the other two over to an almost flat topped boulder a distance away from the rest. 'Give me that parcel.'

Slim handed it over. Kale produced a wicked-looking bowie knife from a sheath beside his gun holster and cut the string.

'All the slugs you asked for,' said Slim. 'That baccy an' the socks are mine.' He took them.

Kale took out the bolt of cloth. 'I told yuh to get black,' he said.

'I couldn't see any black. That's dark grey. Ain't much difference.'

'You've got a tongue, ain't yuh?'

'Didn't ask too many questions. Didn't draw attention to myself — like you said.'

Kale leaned closer suddenly. '*Tequila*. You didn't draw attention to yuhself — but you stopped to have a drink.'

'Just one.'

'Can't you ever learn to obey orders?' Kale's deep voice was ominous.

'When we're doin' a job I obey 'em. You ain't got any complaints about that, have yuh? But I ain't a baby. I kin look after myself.'

'Yuh just like to be hornery, don't yuh? Yuh like folks to look at that purty face o'yourn — they cain't do yuh any harm can they? By God, I oughta turn you over to the boys . . . '

'You wouldn't do that, Jack.'

'Cain't afford to right now. But watch yourself, Slim. You're a good boy but don't think you're too good. Remember what happened to Sansome.'

'Bo was a yeller rat.'

Kale rose. 'Yeh. Bo was a yeller rat.' He led them over to the group. All the time Brodie had not spoken a word. He looked at Slim and Slim winked.

The three of them sat down with the

group, who let up on their card-playing.

'Everythin' awlright?' asked one man.

'Yeh, rest easy,' said Kale.

Slim took out his new pack of tobacco and broke the seal. From another pocket he took a small wash-leather bag. It already held cigarette paper. He transferred the baccy to it too and handed the 'makings' around. While the men were helping themselves he took off his riding-boots, revealing a pair of socks from which most of his toes and the whole of his heels protruded in grimy splendour. The man next to him held his nose in mock disgust.

Slim removed these apologies for socks and tossed them over his shoulder into the trees behind. He produced his new ones.

'Take a look at these for fancy duds,' he said as he put them on.

He sat wriggling his toes. He received his 'makings' back, with a wry grimace at the slenderness of the pack and rolled himself a quirly.

Kale said: 'What kinda folks did you

see in Jonestown? Many of the mine workers hangin' around?'

'Nope, none at all, 'pears like they got a settlement of their own — lots o' tin shacks down by the mine. The towns-folk are a kind of a sleepy-lookin' lot.'

'Don't let 'em fool yuh. They're small-holders scratching a living. They're suspicious an' mean an' dirty.'

'You don't like smallholders, do yuh, Jack?'

'My paw was a smallholder. He worked my maw to death an' tried to do the same for me, scratchin' from mornin' to night, an' not enough to eat most o' the time, because he hadn't got the guts to try anything else.'

'You shore hated your ol' man.'

'Hated him! By God, I killed him — it was the finest thing I ever did. An' every time I kill a no-good man now it's like I'm killing my paw all over again . . . ' Kale's voice died and there was a strained silence.

An evil-looking oldtimer opposite said: 'Did you hate your paw, Slim?'

Slim looked up. 'You know damwell I didn't have a paw, Smoky.'

'Naw, you wuz found under a prickly pear, warn't yuh?'

'You know I never knew my father. You know what I am as well as I do, but yuh don't have to keep reminding me of it. I'll . . . '

'Easy, Slim,' said the younker's neighbour, resting a hand on his arm.

Slim subsided, muttering a little under his breath, his lower lip more petulant than ever.

In the distance came the hoot of a train whistle. Jack Kale said:

'There goes the bullion-train — tho' it ain't got a helluva lot of bullion in it this time I'm figurin' — complete with guards. Tomorrer it'll return with the same guards; but they'll be kinda drowsy after their night in Tucson I guess. An' you all know what'll be on that train, don't you?'

'Shore thing . . . ' The boys laughed.

'How exactly air yuh aiming to swing it, Jack?' said old Smoky.

2

It was evening when Thaddeus Jenkins rode into Jonestown. The peaks were crimson with the dying sun and the treacherous desert looked a restful place. From the direction of the miners' settlement, which was spread like the beginnings of a rash at the base of the Devil's Fingers, came the sound of music. The gusty, dusty wind played strange tricks so that the sound came in weird snatches, like echoes from a far-off sphere.

Anna Mowbray was putting up the shutters at the shop window when Jenkins dismounted from his horse and strode on to the boardwalk behind her.

'Are yuh closing, miss?' he said.

She turned towards the tall, well-built man in the gloom. 'I was. But can I get you anything before I do?'

'That's mighty kind of you, miss.

There are one or two little items I would like.'

'Come inside,' she said.

At the counter, beneath the hanging hurricane-lamp, she turned to him. Her face was illumined; the glossy mass of her black hair. Little wonder that Jenkins stopped in his tracks, himself shielded by the soft gloom, and looked at her.

'Yes?' she said.

He came forward then. 'I'd like some forty-five shells,' he said. 'That's the most important — don't do for a man to walk around with an empty gun an' no shells in his belt. I want some smokes too an' a new kerchief, but if you cain't get at 'em right now they can wait till morning.'

'I can get them,' she said. It was inevitable that, looking at this stranger with the hard, mahogany face, she should think of the other stranger who had called that morning — and also asked for ammunition and smoking gear. He had been young, as young as

16

herself. This one was older, almost old enough to be her father maybe. But there was a similarity about them, the same hard, untamed look, only this one did not flaunt it as the other one had.

She gave him what he wanted: he chose a kerchief of sombre hue to match the rest of his clothing which was a mixture of navy blue and dark grey. While he waited for his change he thumbed shells into his gunbelt and into the chambers of the shiny walnut-handled Colt, doing this with a grave, interested face almost as if the girl was not there anymore.

When she gave him his change he looked up and said 'Thank you, miss,' and then he smiled. It was a rather shy smile, breaking slowly as if rarely used and deepening the lines in his face and around his deep-set eyes. As he left, the girl was thinking of the other smile — the one she had received that morning from the young man.

As she went out to finish screwing up the shutters her father appeared.

'Who was that?' he said.

'A stranger.'

'Another one? What kind of a stranger?'

'Seemed all right. Looked like a law-officer to me.'

'What made you think that?'

'Oh, just something about him.'

'What would a lawman be doing here?'

'Maybe he's got business at the mine.'

'Which way did he go?'

'I didn't spy on him, father . . . But I think that's his horse outside Kavanaugh's place. The big grey.'

'Fine-lookin' piece of horseflesh,' said her father. They finished fixing the shutters and went in together.

Meanwhile this second stranger of the day — third to Kavanaugh and his minions — was ordering a whisky. Serving at the bar was Kavanaugh's sidekick, Rollo Benson, wearing his perpetual scowl. With ill-grace he gave the stranger his drink and his change.

The tall man did not seem to notice his demeanour, in fact he hardly seemed to notice him at all. Nor did he seem to notice the curious glances that were thrown at him. His face was expressionless, he seemed to be cut off from everything and everybody, as he stood with one foot on the brass rail and took a sip from his drink.

Then he threw back his head and drained the glass, looked up, said, 'Give me another one, friend.'

Rollo, who was serving somebody else, passed the stranger without a glance. After serving the customer he went on to the other end of the bar.

He stopped dead when he reached there. The stranger had changed places. He leaned across the bar and looked up at Rollo and smiled gently.

'More whisky, friend,' he said. 'I'm kinda dry.'

The barman looked for a moment deep into dark eyes; there was nothing in those depths; no friendliness, no nothing. They gave Rollo the creeps.

'Yes, suh,' he said. He raked a half-bottle from under the bar and broached it. 'Take what you want. Pay me later.'

'Thank you, friend,' said the stranger.

Rollo attempted to twist his scowl into a smile. He looked like a sick cow. He passed along the bar.

When he came nearer the stranger again he noticed that the contents of the whisky bottle were somewhat depleted. A hand came out and hooked his arm.

'I would speak with you, friend,' said Thaddeus Jenkins.

'Yeh?'

'It is maybe that I shall stay in this town a few days. Could you find me a room?'

'There ain't no more'n two rooms here, mister. We don't get many stayin'-visitors. I'll ask the boss.'

He shuffled off and, in a few moments returned with Sam Kavanaugh.

So it was that Thaddeus Jenkins, after Sam had appraised him and had a few words with him, got himself a room at Kavanaugh's Bar.

Sam Kavanaugh was a wise and diplomatic man. This stranger looked like a square-shooter — but one never could tell. Sam had more sense than to ask questions right then: he learned the stranger's name was Jenkins, figured by his talk that he came from Texas, told him to make himself comfortable and left him to his drinking.

Sam's seemingly friendly acceptance of the newcomer made the habitués of the saloon more suspicious than ever. They were a lean, dark, hard-looking lot, but the stranger took no more notice of them than if they were a row of dummies. He did not look sullen as the one-eyed man had this morning — or arrogant and defiant like his young pard. There was a natural poise about him that had nothing to do with arrogance or any other pose, but was rather the fruits of experience with many men in many places — until men, gathered together in bunches in tinpot

21

towns like this one, failed to interest him any more.

These men in Kavanaugh's place were not mean or bad at the best of times: it was just that for so many years they had fought this dry, treacherous country, the Apaches it spawned, the fugitives in search of hiding, the dust storms, the drought, that they had begun to become like it themselves, hard, merciless, holding on to what they had tooth and nail, resenting instinctively any visitor from the outside world. They hated the mine people, and had the latter not their own settlement, there would surely have been trouble. There were rumours that the Chicago business man who owned the mine was talking about opening up in other places in the territory — and was it not possible that he might encroach on the fields they had tilled and planted?

Consequently all strangers were suspected and hated. For the most part it was a passive hate, for dogged men like these let things simmer and were not easily roused. There were exceptions, however — and the chief among them was Red Porter.

Red was six-foot four in his socks and broad as a barn door. He had a face like something chipped out of the solid rock of the Devil's Fingers; and the whole was topped by an unruly thatch that flamed like a summer sunset.

Red had been advocating an attack on the mine for a long time. Show 'em what's what before they start to spread, he said; before they got too strong and started to tear the land apart. But you can't attack people for just nothing: so Red ranted in vain.

Red, who was the worst farmer of the bunch and spent more time in the saloon than he did on his land, had seen the two strangers of the morning. To him they were pizen: all strangers were pizen. But he let those two go without a comment. And now here, the very same day, was another one. It seemed to the big fellow, who was by now pretty drunk, that he was being spied on. All these strangers had been sent from the mine to spy on him. They knew he was the one who carried the most weight in this territory, would be leader if it came to a fight, and they wanted to see just exactly what they had to contend with. By God, he'd show 'em.

He emitted two explosive words, 'Damn strangers!' and rose from the table where he sat with three of his cronies.

'What's eatin' yuh, Red?' said one of them. But the big fellow did not heed him, he was already bumbling across the room.

He finished up side by side with the stranger and looked into his face.

'What's yuh business in this town, mister?' he said.

Thaddeus Jenkins tilted his eyes up to the craggy, choleric face above him. He was tall, but Red topped him by at least three inches. Jenkins saw trouble in the piggy little eyes with bile spitting in them like fat in a hot pan. He said:

'Who are you?'

'I'm the one who's askin' the questions, mister.'

'Are you the sheriff?'

'We ain't got a sheriff. But I'm the boss around here.'

'You answered that question anyway.' Jenkins bowed slightly. 'Thank you, friend.'

'Cut out the fancy talk. What're yuh doin' here?'

'I only answer that question to people in an official capacity who have some valid reason for asking it. And then, mark you, friend — and then only when I'm asked in the politest tones.'

Red's huge, square face went almost purple. His voice rose to a bellow. 'Don't back-chat me, fella. I'm boss around here I tell yuh. When I ask questions, folks answer 'em. I don't go for no damn tenderfoot tryin' to outsmart me.'

Heads turned, folks stood up. The things Red had said were not strictly true: tho' many men there were scared of him. When he was in a mood like this he was indeed fearsome, all the bile of months bubbling to the surface. He was mean, cruel, killing mad. If the fool stranger did not placate him somehow Red would tear him apart — treat him like he treated that mining engineer five weeks ago, the gink who had fancied himself as a gunman.

But Red's roar, instead of scaring the soft-spoken stranger, seemed to have aggravated him instead.

His voice rose to a shout, and it had an almost authoritative ring in it that made some of the older men think of a parade ground.

'Who the hell do you think you're bawling at, you blown up bag of wind?'

Red rocked on his heels a little as if the man had struck him across the chops with a quirt. There was a general scramble for cover. Red went for his gun.

He was fast: he had his gun out when the stranger's arm came around, and a bunched fist hit Red's wrist with a soft thud. It was a calculated blow, a scientific, paralysing one. Red's finger contracted on the trigger and the slug almost took one of his own toes off before burying itself in the floor.

Thaddeus Jenkins' other fist came out in a short-arm jab — plumb in Red's liquor-bloated middle. Red gulped and doubled a little. His gun was twisted out of his hand and tossed over the bar, another fist — the stranger seemed to have above his fair share of them — exploded on his chin and he went backwards.

He fell on top of a chair, crushing it like matchwood beneath him.

A couple of his pardners started forward. 'Hold it,' rapped Jenkins. His gun was out now. His lean, broad shouldered body seemed to be quivering with rage, but there was no sign of it in his face and his gun-hand was steady as a rock.

'Stay where you are,' he said. 'I came in here minding my own business, interfering with nobody. The big feller started the ruckus, let's see if he's aimin' to finish it.' Then as one more bolder than the other made another step. 'By God, I'm warnin' yuh — another move like that an' I'll let you have it. Back up. Back, I say, back.' His voice cracked like a whip.

They backed this time. They knew the man meant what he said. There was something now in those dark, deep-set eyes which made them realize how close they were to death. Here was a man who would kill easily and without compunction if he was provoked. He was provoked now and Red's three pals watched him with eyes that suddenly glowed shiftily as they backed.

'That's far enough,' rapped Jenkins. 'Stay right there. I ain't aimin' to get shot in the back by one o' you skunks.'

'That ain't gonna happen here, stranger,' said a dark, emaciated man nearby.

'The stranger's right,' said a cracked old voice. 'Red started it. Let him finish it — he's big enough.'

There were murmurs of assent from the crowd. Hornery and suspicious they might be, but the majority of them were not the sort to gang up on a man who showed he had guts.

The big fellow was rising now. He had sobered up and was fighting mad. But canny too. He rose slowly, his little eyes searching until they rested upon the other man, who stood waiting. Red rested his hands on the floor in front of him and hauled himself up like a grizzly bear.

'Shall I hold your gunbelt, stranger,' said the dark, emaciated man beside Jenkins.

Thaddeus Jenkins turned his head. He saw the narrow, hollow-cheeked face, looked deep into eyes that had seen much misery and pain, and experienced it too. He unbuckled his gunbelt and handed it over. He was turning again when Red launched himself across the room.

Jenkins threw up his fists, tried to side-step. His one blow missed Red entirely, the next one only grazed his face. Then Red's fist hit his shoulder, his weight followed it and Jenkins went back against the bar, hard. A painful 'Ouf' was forced from his lips.

Red tried to hold him with one arm while he raised his fist like a hammer for the finishing blow. Jenkins was no respecter of person: he brought his elbow up suddenly and the sharp point of it jabbed cruelly at Red's adam's apple. The big man gulped with pain, his mouth flying open. By pure reflex his fist came down: it tore a strip of skin from Jenkins' cheekbone.

The stranger had more room: he dropped his fists lower, punishing Red's middle once more. Gurgling a little, Red used his weight, leaning on the man, trying to get his arms around him. But the brief respite had given Jenkins his chance. He sagged at the knees, rammed another right to Red's middle, then ducked loose.

The big man turned on him again — only to receive a haymaker full in the mouth. His bootheels screeched, he held himself up with one hand on the bar.

Jenkins came on; his face was streaked with blood, his eyes blazed. Red launched himself from the bar. There was the sickly sound of flesh meeting flesh. The crowd went 'o-ooh.' Then both men were down, threshing, flailing. For a moment it was hard to tell which was which. Then Jenkins rolled clear; Red on all fours after him, his face bleeding now, red hair like dyed straw across his forehead. His shirt was torn away from one bulky muscular shoulder.

Jenkins pushed a chair in the way of the big man's approach then he hauled himself to his feet. Red, at a disadvantage now, began to rise. Jenkins danced around to him, waited for him, until he was on his feet, head down charging once more, then he danced aside, bringing his fist around and down. It seemed to explode at the base of Red's bull neck. He went down with a terrific thud, flat on his face.

The crowd rumbled and shifted.

'I guess that's taken care o' Red,' said the old cracked voice from the back.

But it had spoken too soon: Red was rising again. Slowly, like a half-stunned buffalo — after a blow that might have killed a lesser man. There was something like wonder in Thaddeus Jenkins' face as he watched him. There was grudging admiration there too.

He was a sporting kind of gent. He stood with his hands dangling, his chest heaving and waited for his opponent to get on his feet.

In time Red reached his feet, shaking his huge leonine head like a wounded animal. His eyes shifted and peered from beneath his thatch. He began to shuffle forward slowly, half-crouching, as if the stranger's last blow had deformed him, his arms crooked a little in front of him, his fingers like talons. He was an awe-inspiring sight now, a primitive creature ready to rend and tear. Jenkins circled away from him warily, moving on the balls of his feet.

Red padded flat-footed. He had learnt his lesson: he intended to rush no more. He would stalk this man like an animal, corner him and grab him, break his arms, break his neck.

They moved in a circle, round and round. The stranger darted in, swinging a punch. Red swayed backwards, tried to grasp the swinging arm. There was a tearing sound and he was left with a strip of cloth in his clawed fingers.

In the crowd somebody laughed nervously. Red heard it. He gave a bellow and lashed out, tigerishly, hand still only half-clenched. Jenkins was not expecting that one. He back-pedalled quickly, too quickly. The calves of his legs came up against an overturned chair and he almost lost balance. He twisted his body and avoided the chair. The crowd was right behind him now, he back-pedalled again as Red came on, then he stopped short. He feinted, then, as Red swerved, flung a low blow. Red gasped as it connected below his heart.

But it was a little more than a gasp of rage. He advanced again, hands reaching.

Jenkins swerved, brushed the crowd, his back to Red's three cronies. One of them stuck out a foot. Jenkins went backwards over it, clutching at air. He hit the floor with a thud. Red charged, pulled up short with a screeching of bootheels, swung a heavy boot. Jenkins jerked his head aside from a blow that would have finished him. But, although the broad toe did not connect, the heel did — with a sickening smack.

'*You bastards*,' yelled the man who held Jenkins' gunbelt. 'Get away from him. Get away I say, or by God I'll drill yuh.'

Red and his three pards backed slowly.

3

The men dozed, spread out through the length and breadth of the long carriage. Most of them had a seat each and were stretched out upon it. One lay on the floor asleep and snoring with his mouth open, his head on a bulging war-bag, an empty whisky bottle by his side. Another man was propped up against a door at the end and taking swigs from a bottle from time to time. In a corner four men were playing cards, in a sleepy fashion, on an outspread blanket.

At opposite sides of the carriage two men were yelling at each other, talking about what they had done in Tucson last night, the liquor they had drunk, the girls they had slept with.

'Sleep, hell,' bawled another man. 'You didn't get no sleep. Dry up now will yuh an' let's have a snooze while we've still got a chance.'

Somebody threw a boot haphazardly. It landed on the stomach of the snoring man. He went 'Ouf' and woke up, reaching for his gun. His holster was twisted, trapped beneath his body. While he rolled over in panicky haste, trying to reach the weapon, everybody else laughed.

He realized where he was. 'Jackasses,' he snorted and went back to sleep.

Many more began to follow his example. Every now and then a man burst out laughing at a funny magazine he was reading — until somebody tore it out of his hand and tossed it across the carriage. Somebody else caught it; it passed from hand to hand while its owner cursed and rose. He sank back into his seat however, and the tattered magazine reposed unwanted in a corner. Somnolence took over.

The whistle beeped and the train rocked on a corner. Then suddenly a terrific shudder went through the whole length of it, jerking men upright in their seats, rolling others pell-mell onto the floor. The brakes screeched and groaned and the train rattled in agony, as if it would fall apart.

A man looked through a window, rubbing his eyes. Then he turned, his mouth yammering.

'There's men comin'. It's a hold-up.'

The door against which a man was leaning was flung open. The man fell on his back. A masked figure stood there, guns levelled. The man on the floor, clutching wildly at thick legs, received a kick in the face which laid him low again.

Two men nearby went for their guns. The masked man's Colts boomed and flamed. One man screamed, clutching at his chest, his eyes wide. He tottered, went down. The other spun on his heels, clutching at his shoulder. His gun clattered to the floor. He leaned over a seat, his face yellow; blood dripped through his fingers and ran down his arm.

'That'll be enough o' that,' said a voice. Heads turned. The other door was open, another man stood there, a shotgun in his hand. Somebody moved. The man's teeth were bared suddenly, eyes flashed through holes in the dark mask. The shotgun boomed. It was carnage as men screamed, wavered, fell in the smoke and the noise. Then the blue smoke cleared.

Four men now lay on the floor of the carriage. The one with the wounded shoulder moaned and bent at the knees. Five more men filed in after the man with the shotgun, who was bowlegged and looked old.

The first bandit remained on guard at the other door, his feet astride the man who lay on his side, his face streaming with blood.

All were masked and the last man to enter was tall and dressed all in black. He walked the whole length of the carriage, his eyes ranging the white-shocked faces. He jerked his thumb at one of his comrades. 'Take their guns,' he said.

A man went along the lines, deftly

lifting guns and tossing them through windows, amid the crash and tinkle of breaking glass. The big black-clad man, indubitably the leader, passed along to the man at the other doorway who was lithe and looked young, his mouth hard and sullen beneath the mask, his still faintly-smoking guns menacing those nearest to him.

The big man spoke to the other, who stood aside to let him pass. From up ahead came the sound of more shooting. Through the windows a running man was seen: the fireman, his peaked cap back to front above his blackened face. His mouth open, his eyes staring.

There was another clatter of shooting. The fireman paused, his body shaking. He fell to his knees. He got up again and stumbled on.

One of the masked men in the carriage leaned from a window and thumbed the hammer of his Colt. The fireman spun on his heels; for a moment his ludicrous, black-smeared face was a horrible, accusing mask. His hat fell off as he pitched forward. His body rolled and was lost to sight beneath the wheels of the train.

Men, even in terror, are sometimes foolishly brave, driven to taking almost hopeless chances. As the black-clad man passed through the doorway he obscured the younger man's view for a moment. In that fraction of time one of the train guards acted. His holster was empty but from inside his shirt he produced a knife. He threw it, even as the young bandit yelled a warning. The black-clad man whirled, cried out in sudden shock and pain as the knife gashed his forearm. It clattered to the floor.

The big man staggered aside, leaving the way clear for the young man and his two guns. The foolhardy guard gave a defiant shout and sprang forward. His hand reached upwards. His body was close to the young bandit's as he grasped the mask and tore it away, his other hand tried to snatch one of the bandit's guns.

The other one barked, the sound muffled a little against the guard's stomach. The bandit's face, fully revealed now, was dark, young, the lower lip protruding, the upper drawn back from white teeth. The deepset eyes glowed savagely, then as the guard — his arms wrapped around his middle like he had the stomach-ache — sank moaning at his feet, the smooth face broke into a little twisted smile.

The black-clad man, ignoring the wounded arm from which blood streamed, passed on. The young man looked down at the moaning squirming creature at his feet and said:

'I'll do that to anybody else who tries to be smart.'

'You dirty Injun polecat!' hissed one of the guards.

The young man's eyes glowed. He snarled again.

'Slim,' said one of the other masked men warningly.

Slim's eyes snapped in that direction. 'You damn' fool,' he said.

He took a few steps forward and slashed with his right hand gun at the guard who had called him names. The man crumpled up, blood staining his hair.

'Nobody calls me things like that,' said Slim as he backed to his post at the door once more.

From behind him came the sudden blam-blam-blam of shots, the echoes swelling then fading. The utter silence. It might have been a train of the dead, the motionless guards already dead within it, white-faced, staring-eyed spirits.

The big man in black came back. With him was another man. The latter carried a bulky valise, a steel padlock at its mouth.

'Put it down,' said the big man. The other did so. The big man drew his gun, levelled it and let fly.

The padlock landed a few yards away, a lump of twisted metal. The bag flew open. The big man went on his knees beside it. He looked inside it.

Then he closed it and tucked it under his arm as he rose.

He said: 'Have you searched these bozoes?'

'No.'

'Search 'em then. Take all money — and anything that can be used as a weapon. But nothin' else y'understand.'

Two masked men detached themselves from the group and took a side apiece along the carriage. The guard who had been sleeping on the floor was now squatting on his haunches.

'Get up,' said one of the bandits.

'Go to hell,' snarled the man, now very much awake. The bandit brought up his knee. The other anticipated the movement and grabbed his thigh with both hands, throwing the man. His companion moved in. The guard slung a punch, which missed. The bandit lashed out and connected. The guard went down. The other bandit scrambled to his feet, drew his gun, lashed out with it as the guard began to rise. There was a dull 'crump.' The guard moaned and lay still.

One of the men grabbed the bulky warbag on which the man had rested his head as he slept and upended it. A miscellany of articles fell out. The bandit swept it apart with his hand. There was nothing of value. The man held onto the warbag for use in stashing knives, a couple of derringers, a blackjack, which his pardner had taken from various guards.

There was not much money. 'I guess *they* haven't been paid yet either,' said the big leader. He turned, looked at the young man. 'Lettin' everybody have a good look at yuh handsome mug ain't yuh?' He swung the valise. 'Here, take this an' get out. Join the other two with the hosses. Keep yuh eyes peeled.'

The young killer pouted like a naughty child. But he took the bag and went. The leader moved along and nudged the bowlegged oldster.

'Pass the word along to get movin'.' The man nodded and went.

The two searchers finished their task

without further mishaps.

'Let's get goin',' said the leader. He stood aside, letting the others pass him, one by one. Then his dark eyes, shining through the mask, raked the carriage. He rapped:

'If any man leaves this train before we're out of sight he'll get shot like a dog. I've got riflemen covering our retreat. You're unarmed — so don't be foolish.'

He might have been talking to a class of unruly boys — except that his deep voice dripped with menace. He backed to the door and followed his men.

Through the windows the guards saw them drop one by one from the train and begin to ascend the gradient. Other men were coming away from other parts. One of them turned suddenly and fired two shots. Somebody shouted. Then there was silence again, until the black-clad man's voice was heard as he stood on the slope waving his men on.

The train-guards moved sluggishly, their eyes strained like those of men waking from a hideous nightmare. Those who could not rise lay on the floor just as some of them had lain before the visitation of the terror. But there was blood on the floor now, a faint blue haze and the pungent tang of powder-smoke in the air.

Suddenly a guard said: 'The van. The boys in the van had shotguns in that cupboard.'

'It's too late,' said another.

'Maybe.' The voice was cracked. 'But we can look. We can't stand here. We gotta do sump'n.'

The man left his place and bumbled along the carriage, through the door in which a few minutes before the sullen young killer had stood. Others began to move then. One said: 'They're going into the trees. There're guns outside — our guns, where they threw 'em. Let's get 'em.'

He went through the door. 'Keerful, Joe,' said one of his pardners.

But Joe had already descended from the train, and was running, half-crouching across the cinders. From up above a rifle spat, the sound flat in the still air. A spurt of dust was kicked up in front of Joe. He fell flat on his stomach. Another man appeared in the doorway behind him.

'There's a gun in front of yuh, Joe,' he said.

The rifle spat again. The man in the doorway went on 'It's . . . ' Then he stopped suddenly as if something had stuck in his throat. He held onto the handrail but his hand began to slide slowly as the weight of his body dragged it down. Finally the hand lost its grip altogether and, like a badly-packed sack of meal, the man pitched from the train.

4

Joe turned his head and cursed. Then he looked up the hill to the figures on the rim. He heard the bark of revolvers. Two slugs kicked up the dust close to him. He looked at the Colt lying in the coarse brown grass at the edge of the cinders. He braced himself and dived. The rifle cracked spitefully. It was part of his movement, part of his straining effort, it brought him tearing pain. His hand closed over the butt of the Colt. He tried to lift it but could not.

'That pesky sniper,' he said mildly. Then he died.

Already other men were leaving the train although bullets smacked into woodwork and sang shrilly on metal. One ran forward with short hopping steps for a few yards then, with an agonized yell, fell on his face. Men began to crawl up the slopes like ants, hunting for guns as they did so. There were a few more scattered shots from up above. Then silence as the figures vanished from the skyline.

Inside the train others had reached the guard's van. A man lay dead there. Another was unconscious with a nasty scalp-wound. The third was sitting up moaning with a bullet in his thigh.

The cupboard which had held the shotguns was wide-open, the bullet-riddled door swinging on its hinges. It was empty. Moving up the other end of the short train, through empty carriages and others where guards had been spread out in twos and threes, other men found further examples of the bandits' ruthlessness. Three more men lay dead; two wounded. The rest of them, disarmed, had moved up to the front of the train.

The driver was dead, shot through the temple. The front of the engine was almost touching a huge tree which had been felled across the line just around the bend. How the driver had managed to pull up in the short space when he turned the bend was a miracle. Evidently the bandits had intended to wreck the train to make doubly sure. Although they had not succeeded in this design their coup had nevertheless been devastatingly successful.

The climbers had almost reached the top of the slope when they heard the thunder of hooves.

'They're getting away,' yelled one man in the forefront and made a desperate bid.

He reached the top of the rise before the others did. The others saw him pause there, raising his gun. Two shots sounded. He threw up his arms. His gun flew from his hand. He pitched backwards and the others scrambled out of the way as he fell towards them. His body bumped and rolled to the bottom of the slope.

The others threw themselves flat as horsemen thundered across the top of the rise and guns blazed. Flat on their bellies the luckless guards retaliated.

One oldster whooped as he saw a masked man sway in the saddle. The horsemen thundered on and disappeared. The oldster checked his glee as, turning his head, he saw that his right-hand neighbour was dead. A little further on another man, with a bullet in his shoulder, was trying desperately to rise.

The rest of them breasted the rise as hoofbeats were fading in the distance. The shadows were dark among the trees. The men moved hopelessly, aimlessly among them. They found the marks where horses had milled, the faint prints of high-heeled riding boots among them; a few crushed cigarette stubs. A little higher along the crest of the ridge they found the nest of boulders where the snipers had crouched, the marks of their toes, and a few scattered Winchester shells.

'We can't do nothin' — nothin',' said one man helplessly.

He was almost weeping. The man who had been shot off the steps of the train by a sniper, shot in the chest so that he died almost instantly, was his elder brother.

'We didn't get one of 'em,' he said. 'Not one.'

'I got one of 'em,' cackled the oldster suddenly. 'I a'most knocked him from his hoss.'

'Come on,' said another. 'We can't even hear 'em now. Let's see if we kin do anythin' down there.'

Like men in a dream they retraced their steps down the slope. On their way down one of them picked up the dead man and slung him over his shoulder, another couple helped the wounded one along.

A man had come forward who said he could drive the train if they got that tree out of the way. It was a monster of the wilds, the top of it lying on the other side of the track, half-flattened but still spread widely, with boughs as thick as a man's arm.

At the base the tree had been severed by blows of a woodman's axe.

'They knew what they were doing,' said one man thoughtfully.

Nothing could be found here except crushed cigarette stubs, the ground had been too hard to show the marks of bootheels.

'They picked their spot well,' said the man who had first spoken, a thickset individual with hard blue eyes. 'The only things that ever go through this region is 'iron horses'. Nobody 'ud hear 'em working.'

'D'yuh think we'll be able to move this, Rippon?' said another man.

'Yeh, if we get every man available on this end I think we'll be able to swing it across the track. Then we'll see what it's like underneath. The line may be damaged.'

The man whose brother had been killed joined the group in time to catch the tail-end of the conversation. 'What are we waitin' for?' he said. 'Let's get it moved. Let's get the train movin' again. We gotta get on, to get hosses to go after them skunks.'

'How about Dave, Hobart?' said Rippon softly.

'He's in the van. He's dead.'

'I'm sorry.' Rippon raised his voice. 'Every man here. Look alive.'

It sounded callous. But it awoke men from their stupor. Rippon was a good man. They ran to do his bidding.

Back at the mine, Rippon was a charge-hand. On these guard duties, which up till now had been looked upon as sprees, he was no more than anybody else. But now, in a time of emergency, he took command, and men obeyed him instinctively.

At his orders a line of men got each side of the trunk and a small cluster, himself among them, at its base.

'When I give the word, heave,' he said. 'Then when I say 'right' the right-hand line begin to move backwards. The rest follow — don't nobody let go — I guess we can manage to drop it jest off the lines . . . Ready? . . . Heave!'

There were grunts as the men strained with bent knees and bowed backs. The tree groaned protestingly, the foliage at the other end rustled and cracked as if in anger. Backs and legs were straightened slowly and the tree rose with them.

The lines began to move, the right-hand one backwards. A member of this band suddenly tripped and went down flat on his back.

'For Pete's sake!' said Rippon in a strained voice, for he was helping with the huge butt. 'Hold it, boys.'

The clumsy man rose to his feet. The lines moved again. There were agonized expressions on most of the men's faces now and sweat began to break forth upon their foreheads. The whip-like topmost boughs were beginning to catch now, beginning to cling to the ground like living creatures — refusing to be swivelled around with the rest.

'Don't give up, men,' said Rippon. 'We're nearly there.' His voice was barely audible. He panted desperately with his companions.

The creaking of the tree was like cries

of anguish as the right hand line moved back — back.

'We're — off — the track,' panted one man suddenly.

'On,' said Rippon. 'On.'

Their knees were sagging again, their backs becoming bowed.

'All right,' said Rippon. 'Ease — her — down . . . Gently.' As the tree gradually subsided men collapsed across it. One cursed with a pinched finger.

'You're damn' lucky yuh didn't get worse than that,' said another.

The track was covered with brush-wood. 'Come on,' snarled Rippon. 'Yuh ain't got time to go to sleep. Let's clear this.'

A little shamefaced, men moved towards him again. The track was soon clear, the shiny ribbons revealed. The man who had volunteered to run the train bent over them.

'They're all right,' he said with the air of an expert. 'Pile in everybody.' He turned to Rippon. 'I want a man for the fire.'

'I'll do it,' said another. It was Hobart, the man whose brother had been killed.

He got in the cab with the would-be driver. The rest moved into the carriages.

A few men had stopped there to tend to the wounded. The meagre supplies from the first-aid box had been used up and they were tearing their own shirts and undergarments.

There was a grim quietness about everything now. Even when the engine let forth its first gush of steam and the train began to vibrate with rekindled life there were no remarks — the lives that had been lost on this trip could never be rekindled . . . The train jerked and began to move forward slowly.

It gathered speed, pumping merrily, the wheels keeping time with their own particular rhythm, a sober dirge to its passengers, as it carried its cargo of tragedy to Jonestown.

★ ★ ★

Sam Kavanaugh walked along the landing and knocked on the closed door. A voice said:

'Come in.'

Kavanaugh opened the door and went in. The tall man was sitting by the window, smoking. The morning sunshine made a halo around the turban-like arrangement of bandages on his head. Beneath them, reaching almost to the right-hand corner of his mouth, was a long strip of plaster.

'Oh, you're up,' said Kavanaugh. 'How yuh feelin'?'

'Purty fair, thanks.'

'What did the doc say?'

'Slight concussion. Take it easy.'

'Good advice,' said Kavanaugh. He sat on the edge of the bed. The other man held out a packet of smokes. Kavanaugh took one.

He lit up and took a few deep draws. Then he leaned forward and said

'Jenkins.'

'Yeh?'

'I don't want you to think that them

settlers air a mean bunch. They're not all like Red. It's only that they've worked hard and scrapped an' fought for what they've got.' Kavanaugh paused, as if he could not find the right words for what he wanted to say. Thaddeus Jenkins continued to look out of the window and smoke and say nothing.

Kavanaugh went on: 'They drove the Apaches outa this territory, they built a town, they started to get on top of things — then a smart mining engineer discovered gold at the foot of the Devil's Fingers — that's that cock-eyed lump of stuff tagged onto the end of the Sierra Madre. Next thing we knew the territory was swarming with surveyors and whatnot — trampling all over people's land. There were one or two nasty brushes between them an' the farmers I can tell yuh — tho' luckily, nobody got kilt. Finally these folks packed up. They hadn't found any more gold 'cept that at the Devil's Fingers. I reckon they decided to make the best of it for the time bein' an' pan that. They got all the necessary and brought it along by stage-coach — plus a bunch of tough miners — who started to work on the spot. First of all they started to come here of nights. They drank; an' I fixed up suppers for 'em sometimes. I'm a business man — an' apart from that, as we'd got 'em here whether we liked it or not, I figured we might as well try to get along with 'em.' Sam Kavanaugh leaned forward, an earnest look on his bovine face. 'You see that, Jenkins, don't yuh?'

'Yeh, I see that. Go on.'

'Wal, admirable tho' my friends the farmers are they're kinda suspicious an' narrow-minded — with reason I guess. They figured that the workings at the Devil's Fingers were just the thin end o' the wedge so to speak an' if, and when, the gold petered out there this all-powerful Chicago businessman 'ud give orders to start cuttin' up the land all around. I've tried to tell 'em different — tho' they're squatters an' I guess they ain't got any real right to the land no more'n anybody else — 'cept they sweat blood to cultivate it an' all the rest. Anyway, I didn't figure there wuz any more gold in the territory — an' this Chicago big-bug had had his railway branch line built for nothin' — all the gold he got outa the Devil's Fingers he could haul out on the stage . . . 'Pears I wuz right too.' Sam paused for breath. Jenkins looked at him quizzically and held out the cigarettes once more. Sam dropped the stub of the old one, which was in danger of singeing his lips, and ground it beneath his heel. He took another with a brief nod — not wasting words now. Jenkins took one for himself. They lit up, took a few draws apiece. Then Sam went on, beginning with another pregnant, 'Anyway —

'The farmers resented the miners horsing around in my place which, as no doubt you've noticed is the only place of its kind in town. At first things were just kinda strained, then the miners, who had more money to spend than any hard working farmer, started to throw their weight about. That led to fights. I was scared o' shooting — real trouble — so I asked the miners to keep away. The hornery cusses kept acoming. Big Red Porter licked a whole passel of 'em, I'll say that for him — but he wanted to take things further. He wanted to drive the miners out altogether. Things were getting pretty serious an' I guess the bosses up at the mine were fed-up of having men on the sick list after bein' beat-up. So they got a canteen and bar built down there. The miners stopped comin' into town an' things have been purty quiet since then.' Sam paused. Then he continued almost pleadingly.

'You can understand why the farmers are suspicious o' strangers can't you? The Devil's Fingers mine is peterin' out, like I said it would, the poor ginks are on tenterhooks wonderin' what'll happen next — tho' personally I don't think anything'll happen 'cept the miners'll jest pack up an' go. Don't think all of 'em are like Red — he had no call to do what he did last night. Or them pards of his . . . '

'I don't bear no malice where there weren't none shown to me,' said Jenkins. 'But I allus aim to pay off scores.'

'Yeh, sure.' Sam's voice was anxious. 'But for Pete's sake don't start anythin' else here.'

'I won't unless he does.'

'You gotta get well first. When you're fit I'll tell you where to find Red — if you still want him. He's bin askin' for it a long time. But you'd hafta be careful. He runs a smallholding an' little stock-farm with four other boys. Three of 'em you saw last night. They're a mean bunch.'

'Who was that party fronted for me last night — the doc said he held 'em off with a gun — the one who held my gunbelt?'

'That's Hannibal Crocket. He wuz one of the first settlers here. He helped to build Jonestown — named after an oldtimer named Zeke Jones who died long since. Hannibal's older than he looks I guess — tho' he allus looks sick. He's kinda mean an' hornery at times but he's a square-shooter.'

'I'd like to see him again,' said Jenkins. 'I'd like to thank him.'

5

Jack Kale and his bunch, the masks stripped from their faces now and stuffed into their pockets, rode hard for a time then slowed down.

'We're not bein' followed,' said Kale. 'They've got no hosses an' it'll take 'em sometime to get to town an' get some. We'll make a detour an' lie up for a while in the new hideout in the Sierra Madre.'

'That's right the back o' the mine,' said one man.

'Correct, Benny,' said Kale. 'It's the last place they'll look for us. They'll be expecting us to make for the border right away.'

'Why don't we?'

'An' have the line patrolled by posses on the lookout for us. An' rot in Mexico. Don't be a fool, Benny. From up in that hideout we can watch the mine — I hope to get more pickings from there before we leave. An' no running into Mexico either. Further East is where we'll be goin'.'

'The chief's right,' said the bow-legged oldster, Smoky, sententiously.

'The chief's allus right,' said Slim in a mincing voice.

Smoky opened his mouth to retaliate but Kale beat him to it.

'You were *right* weren't yuh — standin' showin' yuh purty face to everybody?'

'That couldn't be helped. I fixed the one who did it — with a slug in the guts. He's probably daid by now. But Smoky didn't make things any better — jest afore that he yelled out my name.'

'Yuh doggoned . . . ' The rest of Smoky's invective was drowned by another man saying, 'Yeh, he did that all right.'

'I thought I told all of yuh never to use names while on the job.' Kale's wrath was turned on the oldster now. 'You ought to know better, the years you've bin on the owlhoot . . . '

'This young jackass does too much shootin'. He ain't safe to have on a job . . . '

'You mangy ol' polecat . . . '

'Cut it,' snarled Kale. 'Cut it, damn you, both of yuh . . . '

At this juncture they passed into the clump of trees which had been their hideout the day before and gave such an excellent view of the surrounding territory. Kale said:

'We'll stop here a few minutes. I want to fix this arm. I guess we'd better take a good look at Brodie, too. He looks purty bad.'

Brodie, Slim's one-eyed pard had been tied to his horse, the bullet hole in his side wadded with a pad of rag beneath his shirt. He was sagging across the horse's neck and the patch of his face that could be seen was of a soggy grey colour. They dismounted and clustered around him. Kale turned away and went to the flat boulder which had been his council-table the day before, rolled up his sleeve and inspected the shallow knife-cut in his arm. He figured they were lucky — only one man wounded except himself. Not a very valuable man at that. His own wound was slight but he figured he should take care of it pronto. He did not want to run the risk of being crocked at this stage of the game. They had pulled off the job but they were not finished yet — not by plenty they weren't.

As he tore a strip from his shirt and began to bind the wound his eyes rested on the bulky valise on the rock in front of him. A little smile flitted across his dark face and his eyes glowed. Then he dropped his head, paying attention to what he was doing; he figured he would sterilise the wound as soon as they got up into the hills and it was safe to light a fire.

He finished his task and, rising, caught hold of the bag and strode across to the group who surrounded Brodie. They had laid the one-eyed man on a folded blanket. His eyes were closed and he was breathing in painful gusts. Every now and then he twitched and moaned.

Old Smoky said: 'It looks like he's done for.'

Benny, a little man with a scar, said: 'That slug is in mighty deep an', as we go on it'll get deeper. If it was hooked out, the wound sterilised then bound tightly to stop the blood he might stand a chance. He wants restin' up too.'

'An' air yuh' figgerin' we got time to do all that right now Doctor Benny?' jeered Smoky. 'Or would you like we should make a bed up for him here 'fore we go — an' leave you here to nurse him.'

'I wuz just tellin' yuh what oughta be done. But maybe I could bind the wound tighter.'

'You talk too much, Benny,' said Smoky. 'An' you're wastin' time. He's finished. The only thing we can do is put him out of his misery.'

'He ain't finished,' said Benny argumentatively, while Brodie, who maybe had heard the oldster's last callous words groaned louder.

'He wouldn't bawl that loud if he wuz finished,' said Benny.

Smoky caught his leader's eyes. He saw nothing there, no sign one way or another, nothing but abysmal disinterest. The bowlegged oldtimer drew his gun. 'He soon will be finished,' he said.

A hand came from behind Smoky, grabbed his arm, jerking it up and back.

'No yuh don't,' said the voice of Slim.

Smoky twisted around to face the young man and tried to bring his gun down. Slim held on. Smoky glared.

'Leggo, yuh young jackass,' he said. 'Whadyuh think you're playin' at?'

Nobody else did anything. A faint smile crossed Jack Kale's face as he watched.

Old Smoky glared impotently into the other's eyes; Slim's left hand held his gun-arm, held it up so that the muzzle of the weapon was pointed at the sky. Slim's right hand was hooked into his belt very near his own gun. Slim's face was expressionless. There was that strange glow in his eyes again.

Facing such arrogance Smoky looked suddenly very old, rather like an old enraged turkey-cock, blowed-up but impotent. Slim suddenly let go his hold with a jerk; Smoky's arm wavered, then dropped to his side. The gun hung there laxly.

'Whadyuh think you're playin' at?' the oldster said again. His wrinkled face was very red, even with its tan, he shifted from one foot to the other. His head was thrust forward on his scrawny neck, his little rimmed eyes were bloodshot and shifty. He was trying to whip his rage to a frenzy, trying to whip up enough bile to be able to raise the gun and press the trigger, to blast this hateful young cock-alarum out of his path forever.

But he was old, and he was slower than he used to be, and he was not sure he could make it — or even if he got the first shot in, make it bad enough. The kid's hand was near his gun and he was very fast.

It was almost as if he wanted the old man to move quickly, to lift his gun. And the old man was afraid.

For a very short time they stood, time measured in no more than a second, the old man shifting his feet a little, the young one motionless. A mere moment had passed since the old man's reiterated sentence had died, and gone unanswered, when Jack Kale said:

'Yeh, what *are* yuh playin'at, Slim. Have yuh gone soft. What has gotta be done, *has* to be done you know that.'

'Him! He shoots men down like dogs,' said another fellow at the back of the group, the voice dying as the leader's hawk-like eyes were turned in the direction from whence it came.

Slim did not speak and Smoky, his tension broken now, found his voice once more.

'He's jest doin' it tuh spite me that's

all. He's allus ridin' me. I ain't gonna stand for it . . . '

'*Me* ridin' *you*.' Slim spoke at last. '*You* ain't gonna stand for it.' His voice was bitter, sneering. 'What're yuh gonna do with that gun o'yourn. You ain't gonna shoot Brodie are yuh? What are yuh gonna do with it?' Slim's hand caressed the butt of his own gun now.

Smoky's eyes shifted. 'I'll shoot Brodie if Jack says so.'

'I ain't gonna stand by an' let yuh shoot Brodie — he's my pard.'

'You ain't got no pards. You're jest using Brodie as an excuse to start trouble.'

Slim's lower lip jutted. 'You mangy ol' skunk. I'll . . . '

'Cut it.' Kale's voice rang out. 'How many more times do I hafta tell yuh to cut it? God, what's the matter with you two lately?'

'He started it,' said Smoky with almost senile petulance.

'Put that gun away.' Kale told him. 'Benny — bind Brodie's wound tighter.

We'll get him onto his horse an' take him on to the mountains. We ain't got time to do no more.'

The two rivals, young and old, turned away from each other. Brodie started to moan again as Benny went down beside him. It was almost as if the one-eyed man had been lying listening to them haggle over his fate.

Benny inspected the wound, shaking his head dolefully. He tore the sleeve right out of Brodie's shirt, folded it into a pad and thrust it on top of the blood-sodden rag that already covered the place. Brodie's moans became louder.

'Anybody got a spare belt?' said Benny.

'You can have my old Army belt,' said one man and gave it to him.

Benny tore Brodie's shirt open down the front and got the end of the belt inside. He had to lift and roll the wounded man in order to get the belt under his body. Brodie screamed suddenly.

Benny's face became vicious. 'Quit bawlin' will yuh?' he said. 'Or I'll leave yuh.'

A chattering moan escaped from between the one-eyed man's teeth, then he was silent except for hissing, gasping breathing. He was doing his best to be silent under the scarfaced Benny's rough handling, he evidently was willing to risk the trip to the Sierra Madre rather than be left there. Benny tightened the belt. Then with the help of two other men he hoisted the wounded man onto the horse and tied him there.

Kale had mounted his horse and ridden around the edges of the small wood on a reconnoitring expedition. He returned. 'All clear so far,' he said. 'Let's get goin'.' He led the way forward.

The scarfaced Benny turned away from the wounded man and mounted his own horse. He dropped to the back. Out of the corner of his mouth he said to his neighbour:

'Maybe it'd have been better if Smoky *had* shot him.'

Now that his point had been won Slim seemed to have lost all interest in the cause of it being made. He fell into line in the front with Jack Kale and old Smoky. The latter scowled. Kale looked straight in front of him as he rode. He was wrapped up in himself once more, a man apart.

They rode down a sun-baked rocky slope and straightened out onto perfectly flat arid land, a mixture of bare sand, and short brittle brown grass which crackled beneath the horses' feet. They were on the edge of the 'badlands'. To the right of them a drowzy, purple heat-haze hung over the desert. In front of them were the craggy outlines of the Sierra Madre, the tallest ones among them shrouded in purple mist too. The blue sky above all this natural phenomena was flawless, until the eyes reached the aura of the sun, like a glaring brass ball suspended above it all, and could look no more.

This was wild, cruel, treacherous country, ideal country for wild, cruel, treacherous men. Like these who crawled across its immensity now like bugs on a hot plate, small molecules in the limitless universe — which held hundreds of places like this one — yet bringers of so much tragedy and strife.

The ground began to slope again and Jack Kale veered his horse suddenly to the right. 'Follow me closely,' he called. 'Get in line. Below this rise we cannot be seen from the mine where we pass behind it.'

'Yuh know this territory purty well don't yuh, boss?' said somebody.

'I made it my business to know this territory,' snarled Kale. 'If you hadn't got me to lead yuh some o' you buzzards 'ud purty soon get lost — or be swinging on the end of a rope.'

'The owlhoot ain't what it useter be,' said old Smoky. 'You don't get the same kinda people. I kin remember when Black Gomez held up an 'ull town — Lipville in Texas that was — an' milked 'em dry. I kin remember . . . '

'Quit gabbin',' snarled Kale.

'These ol' men talk too much,' said Slim, getting in the last word.

Smoky turned and glared at him but, obeying his leader, did not say anything.

They began to climb again and the Sierra Madre loomed nearer. To the left of them were the Devil's Fingers which hid the mine.

'I think I hear hosses,' said Slim suddenly.

'Hold it,' said Kale.

They stopped and listened. One of the men started to speak. 'Quiet, damn you,' snarled the leader. Then, after a moment, 'It's hosses all right. Comin' nearer too. They may not be after us — yet. But we don't want to be seen anyway. Whip your hosses up, everybody. C'mon.'

He suited the action to his words and quirted his horse savagely. Others followed his example, or rowelled their beasts. The whole bunch sprung forward, like hounds unleashed, heading for their haven in the mountains.

From in the midst of them a thin moaning scream arose, quivering in the air, as Brodie's horse, speeding with the rest, tossed its helpless rider from side to side.

6

After Sam Kavanaugh had left, Thaddeus Jenkins continued to sit by the window smoking. He looked in front of him and there was no expression on his face whatsoever. He was like a man resting in a half stupor after a long and arduous trail. A trail in search of something. And now maybe when he had got to the end of it that something was not there: things had not gone as he had planned, somebody or something had thrown a wrench into the workings. And here the wanderer was, leaning back, saying 'to hell with it all, it will all be the same in a hundred years'.

That was all as maybe: somehow Jenkins did not look like a man who would act that way. There was something about the line of his jaw, the set of his lips, the steadiness of his eyes that betokened him to be a *hombre* who would not let anything stop him, who would go on seeking and fighting until he dropped. And then would crawl and scratch until he died.

In the distance a train whistle beeped agonizingly and, almost simultaneous with it there was a rap-rap on Jenkins' door.

He said: 'Come in.'

The door was opened and the girl from the general stores stood diffidently there.

He did not show the surprise he felt. He said: 'Come right on in, miss.'

She came in and closed the door behind her with one hand. In the other hand she carried a basin wrapped in a white cloth from the folds of which steam escaped, giving an appetising odour.

She said: 'Doc Singleton asked me to come over and have a look at you this morning. He's had to go down to the mine, one of the men has had his foot smashed. I help Doc with his nursing sometimes — I took a short course in

Tucson.' This was dropped in softly by way of explanation. Jenkins said:

'Haven't they got a doctor at the mine?'

'They had one for a bit but he went back East. Conditions down there are pretty bad by all accounts.'

Jenkins changed the subject again. 'It's mighty good of you to call, Miss.'

'Well, the doctor's so busy. I . . . How is your head?'

'Oh, it's fine.'

'I've brought you some stew,' said the girl quickly. She took a few more steps forward unwrapping the basin as she did so. She put it down on the table at the man's elbow.

'Gosh, that smells good,' he leaned nearer. 'Looks good too.'

'I'll go ask Sam for a knife and fork and some bread,' she said.

'It's mighty . . . '

Jenkins stopped talking. She had already gone; the door was swinging gently and her footsteps went with a smart clack-clack down the passage.

Jenkins opened the window and tossed out his half-smoked cigarette. He swivelled his chair around to face the table. He took the cloth away from the bowl of stew and rubbed his hands in anticipation.

The girl returned with cutlery and slices of bread on a plate. She placed these before him and stood watching him as he attacked the meal with enjoyment. She did not seem to know what to do with her hands.

She said abruptly: 'Can I have a look at that bandage? Doc asked me to.'

'Certainly, miss . . . miss . . . ' He paused interrogatively.

'Mowbray. Anna Mowbray.'

'Certainly, Miss Anna . . . Yuh don't mind if I call you Miss Anna do you? That's how we allus address our womenfolk back in Texas.'

'No, I don't mind.'

Jenkins finished his stew and sat back with a sigh of satisfaction. He smiled at the girl. That slow diffident smile that made his hard face suddenly almost kindly. He said:

'Did you make that stew, Miss Anna?'

'Yes.'

'You're a mighty fine cook.'

It was no polished compliment, but just a forthright statement of fact. Nevertheless the girl felt her face suddenly burn. To cover her momentary confusion she started forward saying:

'I'll look at that bandage now.'

He bent his head and she ran her hands over the folds of the white linen, around the edges. 'Does it hurt?'

'No,' he said.

She made another check to make sure everything was right. She noticed that the hair around his ears was dark brown, glinting almost bronze in parts and, in others sprinkled with silvery grey. She straightened up.

'That'll be all right.'

They both jerked their heads up as bootheels thudded hurriedly in the passage. Then the door was thumped and Sam Kavanaugh's voice called huskily, 'Anna. Anna.'

'Come in,' said Jenkins.

Kavanaugh almost burst into the room. 'Anna,' he said breathlessly. 'A rider's jest come from the mine. The doc says will you come right away, please? The train's bin held up by bandits and the payroll stolen. There's men wounded. Doc says bring plenty of bandages and stuff with you.'

'I'll go right away,' said Anna. 'If you'll excuse me, Mr Jenkins . . . '

'Certainly, Miss Anna.'

The girl ran from the room. Kavanaugh remained behind; he was out of breath; as Anna's footsteps faded away he said:

'Good Gosh.'

Jenkins said: 'Sit down.'

Sam flopped onto the edge of the bed. Jenkins watched him, waited for him to get his breath back, to come out with what he wanted to say.

Finally Sam said: 'I didn't come right out with it in front of the girl — right off: tho' I guess she'll find out about it soon enough . . . But there ain't only wounded — there's dead too. I don't know how many but it must be plenty accordin' to what the messenger said. It must've bin like a massacre. The bandits were masked. They got clean away.'

Jenkins rose, kicked off his moccasins, sat on the bed beside Sam, began to put on his boots.

'Hey,' said Sam.

'I gotta ride,' said Jenkins.

'The doc said you'd gotta rest up with that haid.'

Jenkins said nothing to that. He shrugged his broad shoulders into his leather vest, reached his gunbelt from the gun-rail and buckled it on. He ran his fingers along the rows of cartridges, then he drew the gun and checked it. Lastly he put his hat on his head. It was perched there incongruously. He gave a grimace of disgust and tossed it onto the bed.

'Where's my hoss, Sam?' he said.

'He's in the stables at the back.' Sam's answer was purely mechanical.

'I'll be seein' yuh,' said Jenkins and crossed the room.

Sam came out of his half-trance. He leapt from the bed and bumbled after the tall man, followed him out into the passage, not without, like a good hotel-keeper, closing the door behind him.

He pranced around at Jenkins' heels like an eager sheepdog as they went down the passage.

'You shouldn't go out gallivantin' with yuh haid like that. I'd let yuh have all the news.'

To the back door he followed the tall man, then he let him go. He stood watching him as he saddled his horse and rode out with a wave of his hand. He did not wave in return, his bovine features wore an uncertain look now, there was a hint of suspicion in his pouched watery eyes.

* * *

Thaddeus Jenkins rode up the alley beside Kavanaugh's Bar and out of the main drag. As he went down the street Anna Mowbray came out of the stores and mounted a paint pony at the hitching-rack.

She did not notice the man until they almost met in the middle of the street. Her mouth gaped a little foolishly, giving her the look of a surprised pretty child.

'Mr Jenkins,' she said. 'You shouldn't be out.'

A smile flitted across his face. 'That's what Sam says, Miss Anna. But I've got to go down to the mine.' His face hardened again then and she knew it was no use arguing with him. Anyway, he was plenty big enough to look after himself.

He said: 'Do you mind if I ride along with you, Miss Anna?'

'No, of course I don't.'

By tacit agreement they set their horses at a gallop and were silent as they thundered out of town.

Anna's brain was speeding like her horse's feet. She too, like Sam Kavanaugh, was wondering about this tall stranger; who he was, what he was after now. He was obviously not riding out to the mine with her just for the pleasure of her company. It looked like Red Porter's surmise had been correct and the stranger was connected with the mine — maybe was even a hated surveyor. Though he did not look like any surveyor she had ever seen — not with that low-slung gun, that hard, hawk-like appearance . . . And the way folks said he had handled Big Red too.

Maybe he was just another hired gunman. She did not like to think that about him somehow either. Although in his presence she felt, for some obscure reason, vaguely uncomfortable — like a child before a teacher — she had to admit that there was something likeable about him. True, he was a rough diamond with a forthright manner and no scraping courtesy, but hadn't most of her twenty-two years been spent among rough diamonds? — and did not she prefer them to most of the polished gentlemen she had met during her stay in Tucson, where the sons of Eastern millionaires lorded it in the oil-fields?

Soon they were descending the slope to the mine, like a mass of boxes and spider workings at the base of the Devil's Fingers. The train stood at the end of the line, still, unsmoking, dead, and the sight of it made the girl suddenly shudder.

As they dismounted paunchy Doc Singleton ran out to them. With him was a dark thick-set man who said:

'Mornin', Miss Mowbray.'

'Morning, Mr Rippon.'

Rippon looked suspiciously at Jenkins. The latter said:

'Where is the manager?'

Rippon continued his scrutiny. Something he saw made him answer.

'He's just gone into his office. That place over there.' He pointed to a long, low, white-painted shack.

Jenkins nodded and said, 'Thanks.'

He minced across the sand in his high-heeled boots. Rippon followed him with his eyes, noting the build of him, the way he wore his gun, speculating about the bandages around his head. He saw the stranger knock the manager's door and enter. Then he turned and followed the Doc and Anna Mowbray into the bunkhouse.

★   ★   ★

The men rode in single file as they moved into the pass, the craggy walls rising each side of them.

Scarfaced Benny and another man brought up the rear. Out of the corner of his mouth Benny was talking.

'Queer about Kale makin' us wear masks for this job. He's never done it before — not since I bin with him anyway.'

'Nor me. He's kept us all outa sight too, laying-up in the hideout like a lot o' possums. 'Cept when Slim an' Brodie went into town . . . '

'Yeh, an' look how he acted when he found out Slim had stopped for a drink.'

'Slim don't give a cuss. He's as mean as a sidewinder is that younker. Him an' Smoky are shore to have a big blowoff afore long. An' I wouldn't like to be in Smoky's shoes . . .'

'Aw, Slim's jest a blowed-up kid. He don't worry me none.'

'He would if you wuz as old as Smoky.'

'Smoky's still got plenty o' jump in him. He'll fix Slim if the kid don't watch out — throw down on him unawares or sump'n. Smoky knows all the tricks; he might be old, but he ain't no Sunday School preacher. He shore hates that kid like pizen.'

'It's understandable ain't it? Smoky was Kale's righthand man till Slim came along. He's havin' his neck shoved outa joint. Seems almost like Kale's cottoned to the kid — he lets him get away with a damsight more than he'd stand from anybody else.'

'Yeh, I saw Kale plug a man in the guts once — jest for answering him back. He's . . . '

Benny stopped talking as their leader's voice rang out up ahead. 'Look lively back there.'

They urged their horses forward. Up ahead the pass widened, the walls fell away and became slopes sprinkled by huge fantastic boulders. The men spread out and began to climb. After a short time they had to dismount from their horses and lead them, not without a modicum of cursing and scrambling and wielding of quirts.

Their ascent was slow and laborious and tortuous. They hauled on taut reins while horses snorted, their hoofs slipping and clattering and ringing on the hard rock. The rays of the sun beat down and rebounded into men's eyes until they were almost blinded by them. Their faces streamed with sweat, patches of it showed through their shirts, while the flanks and withers and nostrils of their horses were oily and lathered.

On a small piece of tableland they halted. Jack Kale walked to the edge and looked down and around him, a proud black-clad figure surveying a land, which in its tortuous beauty mirrored his own black soul with its striving and its torments.

When he turned back to his men his voice was a rasping snarl. 'Come on; you ain't got time to lay down and snooze.' The men rose to their feet and tugged at their horses. They moved along the table-land a little way and then began to climb again. Once more Kale forged ahead, but Slim pretty soon drew abreast with him, leering back at Smoky who, tottering on his old pins, was gradually falling further and further behind.

'There it is up ahead,' said Kale. 'Around the corner of that jutting-out rock.' He pointed with a gauntletted hand then turned and waved his men on. At that moment he looked a born leader.

One by one they scrambled over the edge of the rise and, in single file, followed Kale. He passed out of sight, followed by Slim, a spindly wisp beside him, yet seeming to carry just as much stamina.

When the others caught up with them they were standing in the huge black mouth of a cave.

'Home sweet home,' said Slim.

'Plenty o' room in the back for the hosses,' said Kale. 'Pass right thru'.'

Each man emitted his own profound or blasphemous expression of thankfulness and relief as he crossed the threshold. The last to enter were Smoky, Benny and a redheaded beanpole called 'Stash'. The latter led Brodie's horse, with the wounded man across its back.

'I told the crazy gink not to haul him all the way up here,' said Benny. 'He's daid anyway.'

7

Thaddeus Jenkins left the mine-manager's office, mounted his horse and set out once more. He veered away from the trail which led back to town and plunged into the scrub-land. He made a wide detour around the back of the town then began to veer once more to the left, keeping roughly parallel with the railroad line.

Behind the town was an area of slightly richer grass and acres of ploughed fields. Farmhouses were dotted over the table-land. There were yellow fields of corn and wheat, shimmering in the sunshine. Here was a monument of man's patience and indomitable will against the forces of Nature in a cruel land.

Beyond this area Nature held full sway again: beneath the purpling haze was a rocky plateau sprinkled with outcrops of sturdy trees. Along there somewhere the train robbery had occurred.

Here and there Jenkins saw men working in the fields. They were like toiling ants but peace hung over them. None of them were near enough for the rider to see them clearly but he saw them straighten and had an idea they were watching him. He wondered which farm belonged to the phlegmatic Hannibal Crocket, who had saved his bacon last night.

He was drawing level with an outcrop of rock which jutted from the grassland and a couple of hundred yards to the left of him when three riders came into view and rode straight for him.

As they came nearer Jenkins recognized Red Porter and two of his pardners. 'Think of the devil . . . '

The three men spread out and half-surrounded the stranger, the big man pulling in right in front of him. Jenkins could do nothing else but stop.

'Wal, if it ain't the durned snooper!' jeered Red.

'I'm in a hurry, fellah,' said Jenkins. 'I haven't got time to bandy words with you right now.'

'In a hurry air yuh? Don't tell me you're leavin' our fair country?'

'No, I ain't leavin'.'

'No, you ain't leavin', you're just doin' what you bin paid to do — snoop around. An', goddam ya, you're on my land!' Red's voice rose to a bellow: he was working himself into another of his rages.

Jenkins said: 'I didn't know this was your land. Anyway, there ain't no fences. I was jest passin' thru'; let me pass, fellah; we'll settle our account later.'

'Hark at him, boys,' said Red. He mimicked Jenkins in a small squeaky voice. '*We'll settle our account later* . . . But that don't do for Red Porter, does it, boys? Red Porter don't run away from nothin'! I reckon now is as good a time as any to settle accounts — ain't it, boys?'

'Shore is.' The boys grinned.

Jenkins shrugged slightly. Next moment there was a gun in his hand. 'Let me pass,' he said.

Porter's face went a shade redder as he guffawed throatily. His little eyes were wary.

'Guns is it?'

'I mean business,' said Jenkins. 'Move.'

Red's eyes flickered. Jenkins half-turned in the saddle. He was not quick enough; one of the men at the side spurred his mount forward: it crashed into Jenkins' horse. The beast snorted; the man reeled in the saddle, his gun waving.

Red took his chance . . . drew . . . lashed out; the barrel of the gun bit into the fleshy part of Jenkins' shoulder. The tall man said 'Oh' and his Colt flew from his hand and hit the ground with a soft thud a few yards away. Jenkins ducked instinctively as Red's gun flashed downwards again. At the same moment the man the other side, a mere onlooker until now, reached out and grabbed his arm — jerked it viciously.

Jenkins toppled; he grabbed too — with both hands. The two men crashed to the ground together — with Jenkins on top. The Porter man cursed and kicked, his arms were pinned beneath the other's bulk. Jenkins snarled with sudden blind rage and, using his left fist like a hammer, struck twice. The man beneath him groaned and went limp.

Red and the other man dismounted. Jenkins rose; his right arm was numb, hanging. He looked for his gun, decided it was too far away, turned to meet the onslaught of the two men. Then his eyes blazed: Red's gun was levelled, he pressed the trigger. Jenkins felt the hot breath of the slug as he dived. Head down, he crashed into the big man, wrapped his arms around his buttocks. They went down together. Red bellowed as his back hit the hard ground — hard. The dust rose in a cloud.

Jenkins was like a wildcat now. He

made no sound. His teeth were bared, his eyes squinted as he beat at Red's meaty face, which still bore painful marks of the treatment it had received the night before.

Red was no silent fighter. He bellowed, and threshed and blew like a huge beast. Jenkins was at a disadvantage inasmuch that his right arm, though he was using it now, had not much power behind it. With his left fist flailing to and fro he slashed Red with repeated blows across the face. But the big man, who had both hands in use, reached out and grabbed his throat and began to force him back . . . back.

The other man, his gun drawn, danced about behind them watching, waiting. Finally he decided he had waited long enough — Jenkins was being borne backwards — his bandaged head was a perfect target. The man danced forward and swung his gun. Jenkins groaned and fell on top of Red like a limp sack.

The big man heaved him off, rolled

him over on his back. His beefy face was streaming with blood and one of his eyes was completely closed, he grunted as he bent and picked up his gun. He rose and levelled it at the still form.

'Red,' said the other man urgently. 'Red.' He reached out and touched the big man's arm.

With a savage gesture Red shook off the detaining hand. But he lowered his gun.

'Search him,' he snarled.

As the man bent to go through the unconscious Jenkins' duds the other member of the trio rose to his feet.

'You got him, Red?' he said hoarsely.

'Yeh, I got him, Cal,' said Red. There was a sneer in his voice.

The searcher strewed objects on the ground. A clasp-knife, a pack of cigarettes, a book of matches, a wad of notes tucked carelessly into the front pocket of the trousers, a new khaki kerchief.

'That's the lot I think.' The searcher

paused. 'No, wait a minute. He's wearing one o' them body-belts with pockets in.' He delved again.

He brought out a scrap of dark grey cloth and a small leather pocket book. Red immediately snatched the latter and opened it.

'Jumpin' Gophers,' he said.

Cal and the searcher joined him. Red opened the pocketbook wide and held it out for them to see. Inside one side of it was stitched a silver badge.

'US Marshal,' said Cal.

'There's a card in the other side.' Red squinted at it, then he handed it over to Cal. 'You read it, my eyesight ain't none too good.'

Due to Jenkins' manhandling Red had only one eye to see through. But both of his pards knew he could not read anyway.

Cal cocked his head on one side. 'It says he's US Marshal Thaddeus Jenkins of Big Springs, Texas . . . '

'Sounds kinda fishy to me,' burst out Red. 'What's he doin' this far West?

103

. . . I don't believe . . . '

'Hey!' interrupted the man who had done the searching. Red scowled and jerked his head around. 'What's eatin' *you*, Henny?'

Henny held up the strip of grey cloth he had found with the pocket-book. He stretched it out with both hands. 'Look at it. It's a mask!'

Red grabbed it. 'Yeh.' He held it up in front of his face, like a child with a toy, looked through the slits in it. Then he waved it in front of the other men's noses like a banner. 'The train robbery! The train robbery that rider was babblin' about. That saddle-tramp ain't no more a marshal than I am — that stuff probably belonged to some poor cuss of a lawman he drygulched. I allus said he'd come here for no good purpose . . . The train robbery! The masked men! Boys, it looks like we ain't gotta go down to the mine to look things over — one of the buzzards has run right into our hands.'

'Certainly looks like it,' said Henny.

At this juncture the person in question groaned and stirred. 'What air we gonna do with him?' said Cal.

The prisoner rose slowly to his knees. 'We'll string him up here an' now,' snarled Red.

The prisoner, resting on one knee now, looked up, focused bleary eyes, punch-drunk through too many knocks on the head.

'Yeh, string him up,' said Cal like a parrot. He had felt the weight of Jenkins' fists and was a little punch-drunk himself.

Henny, the only rational one, said: 'You cain't do that. It ain't safe.'

'Ain't safe?' jeered Red. 'A no-good murderin' saddletramp. Buzzard bait!'

'You gotta take him into town,' went on Henny. 'I guess we kin fix to lynch him there once the story gets around. But it's no good doin' it out here. It ain't worth it. The train robbery's a big thing — I guess the territory'll be lousy with lawmen in next to no time — mebbe this gink can be made to talk.

Take him into town, show the folks you were right after all . . . '

That appealed to Red, who was always glad to show the folks who was right, who was best fitted to be 'boss' of the territory. His brain worked slowly, but smoothly and cunningly once it was on the right track . . . Maybe he'd do even better than just show 'em.

He made his decision. 'We ain't gonna wait till no lawmen come along to make this buzzard talk,' he said. 'He knows where his pards are. What was his hurry, uh?' He paused for effect. 'He was going to meet 'em I guess. *We'll* make him talk — make him tell us where they are — then we'll get the boys together an' wipe out the whole bunch. We'll make folks realize that we don't need no law to take care o' us in this territory. An' thet nobody — big Eastern bugs or anybody — is gonna push us around either . . . '

Jenkins was still resting on one knee, listening, conserving his strength. Under heavy lids his eyes shifted. They

106

came to rest on his gun still lying a few yards away. They flickered the other way to the horses, standing together. The gun was the nearest.

He tensed himself like a sprinter awaiting the fall of the starter's flag. Then he leapt. Even as he did so he realized it was a forlorn hope. Red had moved too: even while he talked he had evidently been waiting for something to happen. They met with a sickening thud of flesh against flesh and the weaker Jenkins went down.

Red sprawled over him, regained his balance. 'Get him,' he bawled.

Jenkins was trying to rise when both Henny and Cal landed atop of him.

'Hold him,' said Red.

The two men held Jenkins, whose threshing was becoming a little feebler. He had plenty of spunk. After a couple of knockout blows such as he had received, both during the last twelve hours, many a man would have been completely submerged.

Red fetched a lariat from off his

saddle and returned with it. 'Hold him damn you,' he snarled as Jenkins kicked out and almost swept his feet from under him.

'Hold his legs, Henny.'

Henny attempted to do so and received a bony knee in his adams-apple for his pains. He gulped and swung viciously with his fist. It sank into Jenkins' lean middle, who went slack as wind escaped from him in a painful gust. Red grunted gleefully and looped his legs, hauling on the rope, pulling it cruelly tight.

'Roll him over,' he said. 'Roll him over.'

Jenkins had gotten some of his wind back. He got one arm free and lashed out. Cal took the blow full in the mouth and went backwards. Henny, still smarting, lashed out and Jenkins took the blow on the jaw. Red joined in and next moment the fractious prisoner was lying on his face. Henny, spitting blood, righted himself and raised a fist above the bandaged head.

'Hold it,' snarled Red. 'Grab his other arm.'

Henny scowled but did as he was told. Between them he and Cal got Jenkins' hands behind him and Red tied them with the rope.

'Now roll him over on his back again,' the big man said. The trussed man was rolled over and lay looking upwards. He did not say anything, but his eyes, squinting in the sunlight, spoke things that the three men could not mistake. The thin firm lips were curled in an ironical sneer.

It enraged Red. He struck out with the back of his hand. The knuckles came away red-stained; a thin trickle of blood ran down Jenkins' chin.

He said softly. 'You'll pay for that.'

'I thought that'd make yuh talk,' jeered Red. 'Talk some more. Go on. Tell us where yuh pals are hiding out. Sing us a song about 'em — all the words.' He was not bellowing now. His voice was soft, laden with menace.

'Better start singin' pronto or, by

God, it'll be the worse for yuh.'

Jenkins said: 'You're makin' a big mistake, fellah — buildin' yourself up a whole pack o' trouble.'

Red cursed savagely and hit him full in the face with his clenched fist. Jenkins' head jerked back, his eyes closed in pain.

'Take it easy, Red,' said Henny. 'You don't want to kill him.'

Through a mask of blood and pain Jenkins' eyes glared upwards once more. The bandages on his head were dirty and askew, the strip of plaster on his cheek hanging loose. Red caught hold of the end of this and jerked viciously. Fresh blood spurted from the reopened wound. No sound escaped from Jenkins' tight lips.

'By God, I'll make yuh squeal,' said the big man, raising his fist again.

'Red,' said Cal. 'There's folks comin'.'

Red let his fist fall to his side, turned his head. Then he rose and, thumbs hooked in his belt, turned straddle-legged to face the oncoming riders.

They came at a gallop and drew up in a cloud of dust: a bunch of farmers, the dark cadaverous Hannibal Crocket among them. Their eyes took in the scene. It was Crocket who spoke.

'What's the matter with yuh, Red? Air yuh goin' crazy?'

All three men began to talk at once. Red glared at his two minions and silenced them. Here was Crocket, perhaps the only rival he had for the post of uncrowned king of the Jonestown territory. Not that Crocket had ever claimed to be king — he hadn't; but he always seemed to be getting in the way of the man who aspired to be such.

Red bawled, 'I told yuh this gink was a no-good. Look,' he held up the mask. 'He wuz a member of the train robbery gang. He's also got a pocket-book an' badge belonging to some pore lawman he drygulched — fellah by the name o' Thaddeus Jenkins . . . '

'That's what he calls himself,' said Crocket.

'Of course he does. It's a dandy front. If he hadn't've bin so damn' foolish as to carry his mask around with him as well he might've got away with it.'

Hannibal Crocket dismounted from his horse and examined the two articles. The prisoner watched the procedure with hooded eyes and said nothing. His face was a mess.

Crocket looked at him, then back at Red. His cadaverous face was troubled. He said:

'You're a mite hasty I'm thinkin', Red.' He weighed the two articles, one in each hand. 'You got a badge an' you got a mask. You'd sooner believe this man is the wearer of the mask rather than the badge because that's the way you want it to be . . . ' The ring of horsemen had moved nearer; they listened closely.

'Aw, hell,' said Red. 'We're wastin' time. He's gotta tell us where his pals air hidin' — pronto — so's we can git after 'em. I'll make him talk!'

'Seems to me you've tried hard enough, judging by the look of him,' said Crocket. 'I propose we take him into town — an' pow-wow things over in a rational manner.'

'Fine talk,' sneered Red.

Crocket ignored him, turning to the others. 'What do the rest o' you boys think?'

'Sounds like the best plan to me,' said another man. There were murmurs of assent. Crocket turned back to the big redhead. 'There y'are, carried by vote: yuh cain't go agin that . . . Help me to get him on his hoss some of yuh.'

Red looked murderous. But he could not go against the will of all of them. 'You'll see I'm right,' he said. 'An' you'll be sorry yuh didn't do as I said.'

8

'We'll take him to the ol' blockhouse,' said Hannibal Crocket as the bunch rode into Jonestown.

'Yeh, an' by Peter, we'll make him talk there,' said Red Porter. 'We've wasted enough time.'

Now a few more voices, including those of his own two men, sided with the big fellow. Everybody was wondering about the stranger, waiting for him to speak. His pose of almost arrogant silence was beginning to irritate many of them.

The blockhouse, one of the relics of Indian fighting days, was at the end of the main drag, back of the town's large corral, and facing the blue peaks of the Sierra Madre and the Devil's Fingers.

A large, square building with thick dobe walls, row of slits for windows — and firing points — and a scalloped balustrade on top of the whole from which to survey the surrounding countryside. This latter also was an ideal snipers' nest. The heavy main door was solid pine, bound and studded with iron. It was discovered to be locked.

This caused a delay, for nobody knew for sure where the key was kept. Tempers were becoming more strained when Lye Mowbray appeared on the scene. He was surprised to see Jenkins trussed up and bloodied like a Christmas turkey, since he had watched him ride out of town with his daughter, Anna, little more than an hour ago.

He began to ask questions but was drowned by people wanting to know where 'the damned key' was.

Lye said: 'It's in my place. I've allus kept it.'

'Get it then.' Red Porter started forward. Things were being taken over by Hannibal Crocket and the big man did not like it. 'I'll come with you,' he said.

A few moments later he returned with the key, the paunchy storekeeper still jittering around behind him like a fussy hen. Red elbowed his way to the front of the mob, which was being swelled now by the arrival of more townsfolk, and inserted the huge key in the lock. With a grunt he turned it. He shoved the door with his shoulder; the hinges groaned agonizingly as the door opened slowly.

'Bring him in,' he shouted.

Jenkins, his legs free now, was half-carried, half-shoved into the interior of the blockhouse.

The place was bare except for benches around the walls, a single rickety table in the centre. Jenkins was slammed down on one of the benches. The bunch clamoured around him. Everybody was getting het-up now.

'Shut the door,' bawled Red Porter. 'We don't want the whole durn' town in here.'

Hard-faced settlers put their shoulders against the door and shut it in the faces of those outside. Henny took the key from Red and locked up again.

The big fellow loomed over the man who lolled against the wall with his hands tied behind his back. 'Now talk, yuh skunk!' he bawled and raised his fist.

'Yeh, come on, let's get to the bottom of this,' said one man.

'Talk, stranger,' said another one.

'Let him have it, Red,' said the vicious Cal.

Hannibal Crocket thrust his way forward — stood beside the redhead.

'Take it easy,' he said. 'Give him a chance to speak if he's gonna.'

He leaned forward to the man on the bench against the wall. His face was hard, his eyes had gone very bleak. 'Listen, Mr Jenkins, or whatever you call yuhself — maybe Red has been rough with you, but we're givin' you a chance now. Your attitude ain't helpin' things none. Tell us who you are an' what you're doin' here . . . '

His voice was drowned then by the

din of the rest. He held up his hands. Slowly the babble died. The prisoner began to speak.

'I'm jest who it says I am in that pocket-book.'

'Awlright, but you're a bit outa bounds aren't yuh? What are yuh doin' here?'

'I guess that's my business.'

'There yuh are,' bawled Red. 'Them's the kind of answers you'll keep gettin' — you're too damn' soft with him. If you'd . . . '

Crocket's decisive voice cut in again. 'What brought you with that mask, stranger?'

'Awlright,' said Jenkins wearily. 'It was picked up by one o' the train guards after the robbery. I had it off Cuthberts, the manager o' the mine. I was going down to the scene o' the holdup to have a look around when those three buzzards jumped me . . . '

'A likely story,' said Red.

Crocket said: 'Awlright. So you're a lawman — you wanted to investigate.

But the train holdup has happened since you came. What brought you here in the fust place?'

Jenkins looked up. He said: 'I owe you thanks for last night, pardner. I'm passing 'em to yuh right now. You're tryin' to save my bacon again. It's mighty white of yuh. But,' he paused, then his voice rose, his eyes left Crocket and ranged the hostile faces around him. 'But I came here in peace an' I've bin bullyragged ever since I came. What I came here for in the fust place is nobody's damn' business but my own — an' I ain't answerin' any more questions.'

'What did I tell yuh !' bawled Red Porter. He lowered his voice, made it squeaky. '*I ain't answerin' any more questions.*'

Folks laughed. Red grinned, showing gappy teeth, very sure of himself again. He turned and held up his hands, quelling the din with a ponderous gesture.

'Why ain't he answerin' any more

questions?' he bawled. 'Because he cain't think o' the answers — because the real answers ain't gonna please us. That's why. He ain't no more a marshal than I am — why would a marshal want to come all the way from Texas to here? — comin' in peace as he says. Pah!' Red spat. 'I figger he'd sing a different tune if I persuaded him a bit more.'

'Make him sing, Red,' said Cal.

Hannibal Crocket bent nearer to the prisoner. 'It's outa my hands now,' he said. 'If you're really on the level why don't you talk?'

Jenkins lurched sideways and said out of the corner of his mouth: 'If you want to help me get the mine manager right away, tell him what's happening, tell him I want the letter I left with him this morning.'

Crocket's deepset, tortured eyes looked deep into the other man's. 'I don't want to leave yuh . . . '

'I'll stand 'em off somehow. Do that!'

'All right,' said Crocket and he turned. As he made for the door, for the benefit of the others he shouted, 'A man's innocent until he's bin proven guilty. I wash my hands of this. I want no part of it. Let me out, Henny.'

Henny, with a sneering smile, unlocked the door and let him out.

Lye Mowbray accosted him outside. 'What's happening in there?' Other townsfolk clustered behind him, all asking the same question.

Crocket took Mowbray aside and spoke to him urgently. The paunchy storekeeper looked alarmed. He nodded his head a few times then ran back to his establishment. A few seconds later he rode a horse around from the back and thundered out of town, bareheaded, his white apron flying in the breeze.

Meanwhile, Hannibal Crocket hurried down the street and entered Kavanaugh's place.

Rollo Benson was polishing the bar. 'What's all the shindig about?' he said.

Crocket did not answer the question, but flung one back. 'Where's Sam?'

'He's upstairs havin' a snooze I

guess,' said Rollo petulantly. 'It'd take a herd o' wild horses to waken him . . . Hey, what's up?' He gaped after Crocket as the lean man took the stairs two at a time.

★   ★   ★

The back of Thaddeus Jenkins' head hit the wall. Red Porter drew back his bloodstained fist once more. The man on the bench sagged forward. Henny caught him.

'You won't make him talk like that,' he said. 'You'll jest kill him.'

There were murmurs of agreement from other members of the bunch. Then they were silent again, unmoving. It was a pregnant silence. This Jenkins had seemed to be a straight-shooter first off. It was not their custom to gang up on a square-shooter. That was the opinion of most of them — as individuals. But now, suddenly, it seemed like they were not individuals any more. They were a mass, a mass symbolized by one gigantic question-mark. There was something fishy about Jenkins, he would not answer questions. Any stranger who would not answer questions was a potential menace. He must be made to answer questions. Many of them would not have done what Red was doing, but they could watch him without qualms, acknowledging him as the leader of this thing (now that Crocket's dissenting voice was removed), placing the onus on his broad shoulders.

Held by Henny the half-senseless Jerkins sagged across Red's arm. With a quick jerk the big man slammed him back against the wall. He sat there, his body upright by sheer sense of will, but his head sunk on his breast, blood from his battered face dripping on to his shirt-front.

'Let me handle him, Red,' said the big man's other sidekick, the vindictive Cal. 'I owe him some.'

He lurched forward and struck out at the figure on the bench. His fist grazed the bandages at the side of the head; they were already askew and blood ran in a thin, spidery stream from beneath them.

'For Pete's sake,' said Henny, standing in the way again, forestalling his pardner's next swing. 'That ain't gonna do no good.'

'It ain't,' said a strained voice from the crowd. 'You'll hafta think o' somp'n better 'n that.'

'I know of somep'n better,' said Red suddenly. 'Somep'n that'd make any man talk — even a bull-headed jackass like this one.'

'What's that, Red?' said Cal. 'What's that?'

'Anybody got any thin rawhide?' said Red, ignoring the question.

'I got a thin stock-riata,' said somebody.

'Get it.'

The door was opened and the man squirmed through a narrow aperture.

'What's goin' on in there?' yelled somebody outside. The man returned with his rope and the door was banged in the faces of the townsfolk.

Red took the thin whip-like rawhide riata. 'Untie the skunk's arms,' he said. 'Hold him!'

Men bustled forward to do his bidding. They were curious to know what Red meant to do next — although many of them had a pretty good idea.

Jenkins was borne back on the bench by force of numbers. His arms were untied. He came alive again and began to strike out, but his arms were soon pinned.

Red looped his legs, as he had looped them once before that morning. He pulled the rope taut and cut off the slack. 'Hold him still,' he said. 'Give me his hands.'

One or two men made objections when they realized what Red meant to do, but they were silenced by the malevolence of the rest. It was as if a devil had entered into them.

Red stood away, his task done. 'Throw the slack over that beam,' he said. 'An' haul him up.'

Willing hands clustered to the job. There was a little milling, a collective long-drawn 'A-ah.' Then Jenkins hung from the beam by his thumbs, his swinging toes just missing the floor.

'They tell me if a man struggles too much his thumbs get slowly pulled outa their sockets,' said Red.

He chuckled. His single little eye — the other was closed, the lid swollen — sparkled with an almost mad light. He rubbed his hands together and even pranced a little bit — as if he had not finished yet, as if he wanted to do something else even crueller, but could not think of it on the spur of the moment.

Jenkins hung limply now, his bloodied head on his breast. He might have been dead.

'Look at me, you skunk,' said Red. 'Look at me.'

The head did not move. With a vicious movement Red grasped the hanging figure and spun it around.

There was a slight sound from up there — maybe a curse, maybe a sigh, maybe a muffled groan.

A voice, high with nervous tension, said: 'Quit it, Red. You shouldn't do that. You . . . '

Other voices drowned his, menacing, argumentative. The men surged around the swinging man.

The mounting hysteria spread. Red was part of it too. 'Will you talk?' he almost screamed. 'Will you talk?'

'Let him hang there till he does,' said one man. 'Come on, boys. Come on.'

'That's right!' bawled Red. 'Run away! Run away like a lot o' sheep.' His voice rose to a scream again. 'I'll make him talk I tell yuh — I'll make him talk.'

Outside the door was suddenly hammered, the blows resounding through the blockhouse. It sounded like a gun-butt was being used.

'Let me in!' shouted the voice of Hannibal Crocket. 'Let me in!' Henny, who had taken charge of the key once more, opened the door. Crocket charged in, behind him Sam Kavanaugh. Both men stopped dead at the scene which met their eyes. Then Crocket whipped out a bowie-knife and started forward once more. With two quick slashes he severed both rawhide lengths and caught Jenkins as he sagged forward.

'Hey!' said Red Porter aggressively. Then he froze as something hard was jabbed into his back.

The voice of Sam Kavanaugh said, 'Keep still, yuh big ox, or I'll blow a hole in yuh.'

Red turned his head slowly and looked into the saloon keeper's face. Sam's usually good-natured expression was missing; there was something like murder in his eyes.

The rest of the company were stunned into silence by such swift action. Then one of them woke up and bawled: 'What's the idea?'

The whole mass of them began to move sluggishly forward. 'Stay still everybody,' yelled Sam Kavanaugh. 'Or I'll let Red have it.'

During the lull Hannibal Crocket raised his voice. 'Listen to me, all of yuh. I've found out that Jenkins couldn't've been at the train holdup this morning. He was in his room — talking to Sam most of the time . . .'

'That's right,' said Sam.

'That don't prove nothin',' said Red Porter. 'He'd have been with 'em I guess if he hadn't've met up with me the night afore. He was sent here tuh spy out the land. He got held up I guess.' Red laughed. Then his face straightened again and he winced as Sam jabbed him hard.

'I'll get yuh,' he snarled over his shoulder.

But his point had been made. Shouting voices backed him up. The lust was on all of them: right then they did not want Jenkins to be innocent, they wanted him to be a member of the murderous gang who had held up the train, for that would justify the things they had done, the things they wanted to keep on doing.

Outside somebody hammered on the door once more.

'Open it,' said Hannibal Crocket.

Mechanically, Henny turned the key in the lock and opened it. Anna Mowbray burst in, stopped on the threshold, taking in the scene before her with wide, horrified eyes.

Then those same eyes blazed and she thrust her way forward. A man got in her way and she slashed him across the face with the gloves she carried.

'You brutes,' she said. 'You filthy brutes.'

9

She went to where Jenkins was sitting on the bench, Crocket standing over him. The latter said:

'You got here quick, Anna.'

'I was coming in when I met father on the trail. He told me what was happening. He'll be back pretty soon.'

She went down on her knees in front of Jenkins. 'Oh, his poor face,' she said softly.

She was startled when the battered figure in front of her said:

'Hallo, Miss Anna.' And it almost seemed like Jenkins was smiling.

'Can you manage to walk?' said the girl.

'I guess so. I ain't daid yet.'

'Come over to our place. I'll fix you up.' She put her arm round his shoulders. He leaned on it a little as he rose: it was warm and soft.

The mob parted sullenly to let the wounded man, and the girl, and Hannibal Crocket pass through. Sam Kavanaugh brought up the rear, an unusual Sam with a gun in his hand and eyes that were menacing. At the door the girl turned suddenly.

'Try and find some shame for what you've done,' she said.

The crowd shifted sullenly then began to drift from the blockhouse and mingle with the vociferating townsfolk outside. Heated arguments arose on all sides; the denizens of Jonestown did not like being kept out of their own blockhouse.

All heads turned as hoofs clattered. Lye Mowbray, his plump face redder than the rising sun, came riding down the street. His white apron billowed, he waved something white above his head.

By the time he dismounted he had quite a crowd around him. Hannibal Crocket pushed his way to the front and took the envelope from the sweating man's hand.

He extracted a folded sheet of paper, flicked it open, and read it.

Then he raised his head. 'Quiet,' he shouted. 'Listen.' Then, as the chattering died, 'This here is a letter from the governor of Texas to the governor of this state; it introduces US Marshal Thaddeus Jenkins, sent to Arizona on a special mission.' He waved the letter aloft, stabbed at it with a lean forefinger. 'Tagged to this letter — an' you're all at liberty to come up an' have a closer look — is a photo of the marshal stamped with a Government stamp, it is unmistakably a photo of that man there.' He pointed at the retreating backs of the man and the girl. 'That man you have mistreated, almost killed, because a big, crazy blowhard told you he was a bandit.'

'You cain't get away with that,' bawled Red Porter. His voice was drowned then as arguments and recriminations broke out with redoubled violence.

Red gnashed his teeth: many of the townsfolk were looking at him with far from friendly eyes. The tide was turning. He decided it would not be safe to pick a fight with Crocket right now. But he'd get him sooner or later. By Peter he would!

'Come on, boys,' he said to Henny and Cal. 'Let's get away from this bunch o' bawling critturs.'

He mounted his horse. His two side-kicks followed him with something like alacrity.

In the soft, comforting gloom of the stores Thaddeus Jenkins said:

'I'm almighty grateful for what you did, Miss Anna. You stopped that mob quicker'n a bunch o' troopers. But I don't want to be no trouble to yuh. I'm awlright — let me go across to my own room . . . '

'All right,' echoed the girl. 'I never heard such talk. You certainly are far from all right.' She was the efficient nurse now, her voice a little sharp, though her arm was tender around his shoulders where it still remained.

'We've got a room in back where I've

nursed more than a few of the pigheaded natives o' this town. I'm takin' you there.'

At that moment her father came behind them, followed by Sam Kavanaugh.

'Take him into the back room, Anna,' said the latter.

That clinched matters. Jenkins did not argue. After the ordeal he had experienced it was pleasant to be fussed, pleasant to be mothered and helped along by a lovely young girl. This store with its magic gloom and its homely smell was like the gentle morning after a nightmare. And above all was the subtle scent of the girl in his nostrils. Not the smell of perfume sprinkled pungently on a painted woman but a fresh, wholesome scent, bath-salts maybe or perfumed soap, like the breath of the sage of his native Texas, refreshing like a sleep under the cool of the stars on a summer's night.

They passed through the trap in the counter, through a door beyond and along a lamplit passage. The girl led him into a dark room and they were close together there for a moment while Lye bustled past them. For the sick, battered man this was soul-stirring magic, making him whole again in body while his mind still drifted in a delicious dream. To feel the soft nearness of the girl and not to see. Not to see anyone else either as if for a pregnant moment of time they were alone together in a dark world of their own which no one else could enter.

The scratch of a lucifer, a blossoming flame, destroyed the illusion and brought Thaddeus Jenkins to sanity once more. A return to cynicism and bitterness and the never-ending fight. The objects of the room were shown into sharp relief, Lye behind the lamp brooding over them like a plump, benevolent genie. The table on which the lamp stood, the few chairs, the huge cupboard, the cot against the wall, the curtains behind woven in a myriad colours, beautiful Indian-like stuff which matched the woven rush mats on the bare polished floor, the counterpane on the cot. Sam Kavanaugh entered the room as Anna flung the counterpane back. She said:

'I'll leave you men to tuck Mr Jenkins in nice and tidy. You can lend him one of your nightshirts, father. See that he gets a wash — treat him gently. I'll be back in a short time to dress those wounds . . .'

'Aw, Miss Anna,' said Jenkins. 'I . . .'

'You must rest, Mr Jenkins,' she told him sharply. 'I want Doc Singleton to see you as soon as he gets back. I don't like the look of that head at all.'

'I've had it a good many years, Miss Anna,' he said feebly. 'Maybe it's gettin' to look a little old and droopy.' The joke did not register with the primly efficient nurse. As she marched from the room she gave her father and Sam meaningful glances. 'Do as I say,' she said.

'Yes, honey,' said Lye. Sam nodded sheepishly. He closed the door behind her. The two men advanced, with dogged expressions, on their victim.

He sat down on the edge of the bunk and held his hands up in front of him.

'Now, boys,' he said.

He tried to smile but only winced instead. His bloodied face was pitiful — it was a little comical too: and the attitude which went with it now.

'Look, boys,' he said.

The boys paused, exchanged glances and advanced again. Jenkins shrugged and tried to grin again. 'Awlright,' he said. 'I give in. I cain't fight the whole town.'

When Anna returned later the patient was propped up in bed with his lean head stuck up comically out of the neck of one of Lye's voluminous nightshirts. His face was red and swollen but fairly clean — though he badly needed a shave. The two men, standing now surveying their handiwork, had not meddled with the grimy, bloodstained bandage askew on his head.

'We'll see to that first,' said Anna.

She placed a tray full of medical-looking objects and articles on the table and brooded over them for a moment like a High Priestess over things incarnate. She had taken off her riding clothes and her shapely figure was clad now in a clean, white apron. Jenkins looked at her back, straight as an arrow, her trim waist, the curve of her hips. Upwards again to the black hair cascading over her shoulders. She was all woman, but for all that, he suddenly found himself shuddering slightly in his weakness. She looked so damnably efficient.

Then she turned and he saw her beautiful, vivacious face, received the full warm look of her dark eyes. He relaxed, more than willing to let her do anything she liked with him.

She removed his bandages and cleaned the wound with cottonwool soaked in some cold stuff which made them smart. It was sweet pain. Her fingers were wonderfully soft and gentle, the nearness of her, the subtle scent of her was like a balm to his senses.

She finished his head. 'There,' she said. 'Does that feel better?'

'Good as new.'

'Now for the face,' she said professionally.

She produced some more cottonwool and a monster roll of sticking-plaster. She began to clean the wounds once more with the icy, stinging stuff. Her face was close to his, her soft, red lips slightly parted; he could feel the gentle warmth of her breath. He looked up into her eyes and saw the pain and the pity in them. Gosh, he thought, he must look a sight.

He sank once more into a delicious stupor while she stroked him and anointed him and plastered him. He was brought back to earth by her voice, like the music of a mountain stream it was, saying, 'You must rest now. Lie down,' and her hands were on his shoulders, pressing him gently. He sank slowly as she took the pillows away from behind his shoulders, punching them, making them soft for his head to rest upon.

'Rest,' she said, and her voice seemed far, far away. He was floating on the clouds.

★ ★ ★

When he awoke his nostrils were assailed by the smell of warm food. A door closed. He lifted up his head. Lye Mowbray was crossing the room with a loaded tray.

'Oh, you're awake,' he said. 'Good. Now I don't have to wake you. Anna said to wake you an' give you some chow. She said it don't do to sleep too long after the beating up you've received — in the haid too.'

He placed the tray on the table. 'If I drag this across kin you sit up an' get at it?'

'Shore.' Jenkins sat up. He winced as a stab of pain shot through his head.

'How yuh feeling?'

'Fine.'

'Son, this town shore gave you a right royal welcome.'

'They shore did.'

Lye dragged the table across. He said: 'Anna said you liked that last bowl of stew she fixed so she's made you some more.'

'It's mighty good of her.'

'She's a fine girl,' said Lye and before anything else could be said on the subject, bustled away. 'Yell out if yuh want me,' he said before he closed the door.

Jenkins attacked the savoury stew. He was a little disappointed that the girl had not brought it herself. Now he felt more rational, and a hell of a lot better too, he wanted to thank her once more. That's what he told himself — he even had a little speech prepared.

As he ate, however, he changed his mind once more. He figured she was not the kind of girl who would wish for elaborate thanks, for fancy phrases — specially from a broken-down old saddle tramp like him. He was over-come by a mood of cynicism and was very harsh with himself. What was the matter with him when he was brought in here? Did he think a sweet girl like Anna was really affected at all by a hornery trouble-shooter like him? Gosh, he must have been really punch drunk! She was a nurse, wasn't she? She'd do the same for any beaten, wounded thing — even a dog! She was that kind of a girl.

He finished the stew and the bread, and the coffee and the sweet wheatmeal cakes. Gosh, she was a mighty fine cook, too. A prize for any man — stuck here with her father in this Godforsaken hole. Why was she? Had she a man tucked away here someplace? Or was she devoted to Lye and unwilling to leave him. She was the type of girl for such unselfish devotion. But she was made, superbly, for other things too; a man, children . . . Jenkins pulled himself up short. What the hell was the matter with him? Had any of the women he had ever known been like that? No! Had he ever felt like that? No! The women he had known had been his own kind: tough birds of passage, living for the moment, loving, and passing on.

With an almost brutal gesture, sudden power surging through his body, he pushed the plates away from him.

There was a knock at the door and he said, 'Come in.'

The door opened and she came in.

10

Her sudden appearance on top of all he had been thinking about her momentarily fuddled him.

'I've brought you some cigarettes,' she said, and put them on the table before him.

They were just what he needed. 'Thank you,' he said. 'I'll have to pay you when . . . '

'You can pay me any time,' she said. 'Don't worry about that, Mr Jenkins.'

He heard himself saying, 'I wish you wouldn't keep calling me Mister, Miss Anna. Cain't you call me Thad? It ain't much of a name, but it's the only one I've got.'

She gave a throaty chuckle. 'All right — Thad. And while we're doing away with titles, you can drop the Miss too.'

He bowed a little. 'Thank you, Anna . . . Thank you for everything.'

'You're welcome,' she said briefly and began to pile the crockery on to the tray.

He reached out for the cigarettes, took one from the pack. She was beside him now, concentrating on what she was doing. He wondered if he had offended her in any way. He said diffidently:

'Have you a match — Anna?'

'Oh, I'm sorry. I've brought you some.' She took them out of her apron pocket and handed them over.

She made as if to go. 'Miss Anna,' he said, then, as she frowned, 'Anna . . . Is there any more news from the mine?'

'You shouldn't be worrying your head over that.' She checked herself. 'No, that sounds callous. What I mean is that you must get well.'

'I'm a lawman, Anna,' he said. 'I must find out all I can.'

'We shan't know anything till Doc gets back,' she said. She turned to go.

He let her reach the door then he called her name. She turned. He said:

'I'm grateful for all you've done for me, but I must tell you — as soon as I can I'm going to get out of this bed. I have things to do — things that aren't pleasant but have to be done. You understand, don't you? You understand some of those things?'

She did not answer right away. She opened the door. Then she looked straight at him again. 'Yes, I understand some of those things,' she said.

She closed the door. Jenkins leaned back and smoked. Another rap came on the door. It opened and Anna's head came round the edge. He did not know what to expect.

She said: 'Doc Singleton's here.'

He said: 'Can I see him, please?'

'He wants to see you.' She vanished. The door opened wider and the fat doctor bustled in. He put his little black bag on the table and perched beside it.

'Well,' he said. 'Let me have a look at you.' He bent forward.

'I'm all right, Doc,' said Jenkins. 'Miss Anna's made a fine job on me.

Tell me: anything new at the mine — any leads at all? I wanted to see where the holdup occurred, talk to some of the men. I haven't been able to do either. I'm corralled here. Give me some information if you can, will you?'

The doc said: 'The manager and Rippon went down to the scene of the holdup. They found nothing — nothing more than Rippon found this morning. The only clue has been the mask that was handed over to you.'

'The mask!' ejaculated Jenkins. 'Yeh. I wonder who's got that now.'

The doctor said: 'The mask was snatched from one of the bandits' faces and a dozen or more of the men saw him. He was a thin younker with long, black hair, dark eyes and a queer little smile on him when he killed a man. One of the other men called him Slim.'

'Slim,' echoed Jenkins.

'You'll be knowing him mebbe.'

'Mebbe,' said Jenkins. 'I have known many younkers called Slim.'

'Some railway men riding out just

before the train got in saw a band of strange riders going into the Sierra Madre. It seemed like they were going into the pass, but when the railway men got there the riders were nowhere to be seen. They must've been making for the border — they must've been travelling fast, too, to get out of sight so quick . . . ' The doc paused.

'You think maybe they're still in the hills.'

'Maybe. And I don't think they were the bandits but prospectors. The bandits would not be foolish enough to come that near the mine — even if they were making for the border.'

'I guess you're right, Doc.'

The fat man rose. 'There ain't much you can do,' he said. 'Best rest easy for a while. I'm givin' you that advice — whether you'll take it or not I don't know. You're in good hands with Anna.'

'I know that, Doc . . . Doc, is there anything else you can tell me before you go. Did any of the men try to describe any more of the bandits?'

'They said the leader was a big man in black. There was also a bowlegged oldtimer with a shotgun. He put paid to two of the men. They were a cold-blooded bunch of killers — the younker and the oldtimer particularly.'

Doc Singleton rose. 'You won't be needing me. I'll get some chow, then go back to the mine. It's a terrible thing that's happened — terrible.' Shaking his head slowly from side to side, he went.

Jenkins' face was very troubled. He smoked until the butt burnt his fingers then he threw it peevishly away. There was another knock on the door and he said, 'Come in.'

Anna ushered in Sam Kavanaugh and Hannibal Crocket. She was turning to leave when Jenkins said:

'Stay here for a bit, Anna, if you can. I've somep'n to tell all of yuh.'

The girl nodded. 'Sit down, gentlemen,' she said. She perched herself primly on the bunk, at Jenkins' feet.

Hannibal walked to the table and put some articles on it.

'Here's your letter, pocket-book an' the mask,' he said.

'Thanks, pardner,' said Jenkins. He reached out for them. Anna laid a hand suddenly on his arm. 'May I see that mask?'

She took it from him and scrutinized it. The three men watched her with avid curiosity.

She said: 'This stuff came off a bale in our stores. I sold six yards of it to a young man the other morning — the same day you came, Thad.'

Jenkins sat up straight. 'Describe the young man,' he said.

She did so. 'Hey,' said Sam Kavanaugh. 'That's the young gink who came into my place — must've bin the same mornin' — he had a one-eye man with him. They drank *tequila*. I guess that's what makes me remember 'em more — I don't sell much *tequila* since the Mexicans an' Apaches moved away.'

'The young man 'ud be the one called Slim, I guess,' said Jenkins. He passed Doc Singleton's information on to them.

151

'They had a nerve coming here getting stuff for their masks,' burst out Anna. She paused. Then she said:

'But that young man — he didn't look like a bandit — he was little more than a boy.'

'A cold-blooded killer by all accounts, whether or not,' said Hannibal Crocket.

'I'd like to say somep'n, folks,' said Jenkins. He paused as they all looked at him and waited. Then he went on:

'You're, I guess, the only real friends I've got in Jonestown. You an' Anna's father an' Doc — an' maybe one or two more. But you're my best amigos.' He paused again. 'I ain't good at speech-making,' he said.

Then he continued: 'That mob wanted to know why I came here. I could've told 'em — if things hadn't turned out as they did maybe I'd've had to tell 'em. But I didn't want to tell them. I didn't want my business to get all over the territory an' maybe mix-up all my plans — such as they were. I didn't know but what any man in the crowd — all of 'em strangers to me — belonged to the very gang I came here in search of. I didn't talk. But I can talk to you in the privacy of this room. I came here on a special mission — hence the letter. I traced a gang of bandits and killers plumb all the way from Texas, where they are wanted for every dirty trick in the book. They blazed a trail of murder and robbery across New Mexico too — everywhere they've gone they've left a load of grief behind 'em. It was a hunch that led me here and I'm pretty certain now that the gang who held up the train are the people I am after. And, knowing 'em as I do, I don't think they have gone over the border.'

'How's that, Thad?' said Sam Kavanaugh.

'I'll tell you,' said Jenkins. He leaned forward a little and his battered face was intent. He looked from Sam to Hannibal Crocket then back again. He said:

'Both you two have been in this territory a long time.'

'Yeh,' they murmured.

'I want you to hark back a good many years and remember a family called Kinsell. A father, mother and son.'

'I remember 'em,' said Crocket. His voice was terse.

'I thought you would,' said Jenkins.

'I remember too,' said Sam. 'An' with good reason. The father was a brute — it was figured he worked his pore wife to death. Then he was killed himself, in mysterious circumstances, and the son vanished. It was thought he had killed his father. Nobody took much pains in tryin' to trace him — an' it was figured the old man had it comin' to him anyway.'

'That youth came to Texas and called himself Jack Kale. He started hell-raisin' right away. He was put in jail for manslaughter an' broke out. He vanished again. He came on the scene again in a gradual way about two years later — leading the murderous gang he's leading now, the gang I am after.'

'The train robbers?'

'Yeh, an' that I figure is why they wore masks. I never heard of 'em wearing masks before. Kale was afraid of being recognized. He wanted to disguise himself and so that none of his band 'ud suspect the reason why, made all of 'em wear the things — as a sort of new innovation.' He turned to Crocket.

'Hannibal, did you know Jack Kinsell very well?'

'Nope. I never had much truck with any o' the Kinsells. I allus thought young Jack a surly brute — tho' he'd got reason to be, I guess.'

'Had he any particular pards?'

'Only a half-cracked kid called Jigger Perks who useter follow him round like a dog.'

'Is this Jigger still around?'

'Yeh, he's bin in town today. He's a grown man now, but he ain't no more sensible than he ever was. What yuh gettin' at, Thad?'

★   ★   ★

155

At the mouth of the cave up in the peaks of the Sierra Madre there was some argument over what to do with a dead body. Brodie was not Brodie any more, he was just an irritating object to be gotten rid of as soon as possible.

Finally Jack Kale discovered a very deep and convenient fissure in the rocks behind the cave. They stripped the body of all accoutrements that might be of use and dumped it down there. They flung small rocks on top of it until it was buried, then covered the fissure with larger rocks.

'I ought to've put him out of his misery back there in the trees like I wanted to,' said old Smoky with a scowl in Slim's direction. 'Then we could've buried him nice an' comfortable.'

Slim did not seem to hear all this so the oldster raised his voice. 'If some folks didn't damwell interfere so much an' try to be awkward. Some unwashed whelps think that they know more than their grandaddies do.'

His words were not well chosen. Slim

heard them. He said:

'I know of a grandaddy who's doddering in his old age and ought to've been hanged years ago — seein' he's no good to himself nor nobody else.'

The men laughed. 'One up to Slim,' said one of them. Brodie, buried like a dog, was completely forgotten.

The laughter rang in Smoky's ears. His lined, mahogany face paled a little. His wizened body shrivelled; his bowed legs seemed even shorter as he crouched.

'Quit the horsin',' he said. 'I ain't standin' no more of it.'

Men moved back a bit, leaving a clear space between the two rivals, the young and the old.

Slim said: 'Yuh shouldn't flap yuh jaw an' try to be smart if yuh cain't stand to be joshed in return, gran'pop.'

Nobody laughed this time. Smoky's aged body quivered with suppressed rage; his face was almost yellow.

'I've stood enough I've told yuh,' he

said in a choked voice. 'I've stood enough.'

'You keep on sayin' it,' said Slim. 'What you aimin' to do about it?'

'Take it easy, Smoky,' said Jack Kale. There was a little smile on his dark face. He moved a little nearer to the two men.

Smoky, his one hand still clawed over the butt of his gun, turned to look at his leader. 'He can't keep hazin' me, Jack,' he said. It was almost a plea.

Kale said nothing. Smoky turned his head again; his eyes flickered in their crowfooted slits. Slim was moving towards him slowly, his thumbs hooked into his belt.

'I'm warnin' yuh, younker,' said the old man.

Then Jack Kale spoke. 'I'm warnin' yuh too. Both of yuh — for the last time.' Like a cat watching mice at play he had given them all the time he could, enjoying the spectacle; now he was calling a halt, threatening to pounce.

Smoky's eyes shifted again, like a dog's at the sound of his master's voice. But Slim did not heed it.

He said, 'You ought to be down thet hole with Brodie, you mangy ol' son-of-a-bitch.' Then he sprang.

Smoky wrenched at his gun. His arm was grabbed, twisted. Then the full weight of Slim's body hit him and he went down with the younker on top of him. He yelled and began to bite and scratch and kick like the old bobcat he was. The men cheered.

Slim was grinning now as he held the old man down, snatched his gun from his holster and tossed it away. Smoky struck up at him, he was almost foaming at the mouth now. Slim parried the blow and caught the old man across the face with a ringing smack of his open palm.

Smoky went crazy then. So violent were his movements that Slim, taken by surprise, was thrown off him like from a bucking bronco. Smoky rose to his knees. The two men met again like fighting cats. With flailing hands the old man kept the younger one off for a time. Then Slim moved through his guard, grabbed the scrawny neck with one hand and hit him twice in the face with the clenched fist of the other. The old man sagged. Slim rose. The men were quieter now.

'That'll be enough, Slim,' said Jack Kale. There was an ominous note in his voice.

The other men looked at him, they were surprised that he had stood it this far. But Slim did not heed him, did not turn towards him. He was watching Smoky. The old man began to rise and there was murder in his eyes. Then they shifted and he saw his gun on the ground. He dived for it.

Slim took a few steps forward and kicked out. Smoky yelped as the toe of the boot bit into his side. He lurched again.

Something flared in Slim's eyes. He was amusing himself no more.

'By God, I'll fix you for good, you

son-of-a-bitch,' he said.

He sprang. His hands reached out and grasped the old man's throat. His knee was thrust into the scrawny chest, forcing Smoky to the ground.

Another hand grabbed Slim's shoulder and he was pulled away from his victim, and sent spinning. He righted himself, striking out at this new enemy.

Jack Kale parried the blow and flung a right which exploded in Slim's mouth. The young man went down. He rose on one elbow and went for his gun.

Kale already had his out. He said: 'That's enough, Slim. Plenty enough.'

Slim spat blood on the ground beside him. 'All right, Jack,' he said. 'All right.'

11

There was a kind of a faraway look in Thaddeus Jenkins' eyes. Hannibal Crocket repeated his question:

'What yuh gettin' at, Thad?'

When Jenkins finally spoke he seemed to be going off at a tangent. His voice was reflective.

'When I was a kid I lived in a mountain district. Similar to this one only not so dry. Like most kids brought up in a place of that kind my favourite game was exploring. Me an' my young pards found all kind of caves an' hidey-holes. I'm figurin' that if I'd spent my younger days around the Sierra Madre I'd've found scores of such places . . . '

'I get yuh,' burst out Sam Kavanaugh. 'You figure Jack Kinsell an' his gang are hiding up in some place their leader found when he was a kid.'

'It's possible, ain't it? I'd sooner believe it than that they've gone over the border. Mr Jack Kinsell, alias Kale, ain't the sort of a man to bury himself in Mexico. I think the bunch of riders the workers saw were the train-robbers an' that they're lying low somewhere off along that pass.'

'It's a mighty long pass,' said Hannibal Crocket. 'Anyway, wouldn't Jack Kinsell figure that somebody else in the territory 'ud know about his hidey hole?'

'That's possible. But don't forget he doesn't know that we know he's Jack Kinsell. You wouldn't have known if I hadn't told you, would you? I guess he never figured I'd tail him this far. He thought he'd left me in Texas — or maybe New Mexico. And, but for the fact that he hasn't, who would know that Jack Kinsell had returned home — and not knowing that the gang they sought was led by Jack Kinsell, who would think of looking for them in the peaks directly behind the mine? Hell, it'd be the last place anybody'd look for them.'

'All you've said is possible,' Hannibal Crocket told him. 'But it's only surmise, ain't it? What you aimin' to do: comb all the peak territory back o' the mine?'

'I'm hoping mebbe that Jigger fellah you mentioned will be able to help us. Can you get him for me?'

'I kin get him,' said Hannibal. 'But whether you'll get any sense out of him is a mighty long shot. By now he's probably forgotten that a kid named Jack Kinsell ever existed. Anyway, if I can't get him before, I'll bring him in tonight for a drink.'

'All right.'

Hannibal rose. 'Is there anything else you'd like to tell us 'fore we go, Thad?'

'No, I don't think so.'

'All right then. Adios.'

'Adios.'

'Adios,' said Sam Kavanaugh and the two men went. Jenkins and the girl were left alone.

Anna remained sitting on the end of the bed. Neither of them spoke for a moment. Then Jenkins said:

'I feel better now, Anna. I'd like to get up. Later I want to go down to Sam's place an' get my gear.'

The girl said: 'If you feel well enough, Thad, there's nothing to stop you getting up.'

'I guess I feel better than I look.'

The girl leaned forward. 'Promise me you won't go out before dusk.'

He looked at her for a few moments. She returned his gaze steadily. Then he said: 'All right. I promise. But I've got a lot to do, you know that.'

'Yes, I know it.'

'If,' he said haltingly, 'if I do things you don't like — I hope you'll realize it's only because I have to do them. I . . . Gosh, I'm getting my tongue plumb twisted in knots . . . '

'Don't say any more,' she said. 'I think I know what you're tryin' to get at. I'll go get your clothes and you can get dressed. Then I want you to sit

165

down here at this table and have some more chow and sit and smoke quietly till dusk.'

'I'll do that,' he said.

She rose and as she did so he reached out and caught her hand. She let it lie there in his for a moment then she drew it away. She left the room.

It was her father who brought Jenkins' clothes. The paunchy storeman said: 'I guessed you wouldn't rest for long. Don't go an' get yourself shot.'

'I'll try not to.'

Lye had gone and Jenkins was fully dressed, except that he was minus a gun and belt, when there was another rap on the door and, at his invitation, Anna entered once more. She carried a loaded tray, an appetising odour issuing therefrom.

She had taken off her white apron and was clad in a flowered dress, dark red predominating in its design, which brought out the lush beauty of her face and form. She smiled with a flash of white teeth.

Jenkins' legs went suddenly weak and he sat down on a chair. Why had his legs gone like that he wondered? Wasn't he as tough as he thought he was, or was this girl bewitching him?

She put the tray down before him. 'Tuck in,' she said 'I'll come back in about half-an-hour's time.'

Then she had turned again. He could not take his eyes off her as she walked to the door. When it had closed behind her he sat motionless for a moment. Then, with a wry grin, he shrugged his shoulders and started on his meal.

When Anna came in again he had finished. The utensils were strewn about on the table before him and he was leaning back in his chair, smoking.

As she began to gather the stuff together he rose. 'Let me help you,' he said.

'You sit down,' she said.

They both reached for a plate at the same time. He got it, she grabbed for it, laughing. He drew it away quickly and it slipped from his fingers and smashed to fragments on the floor.

As they bent down to pick up the pieces they were still laughing. Their heads almost knocked together and their mirth was redoubled. Anna put her hand on his shoulder to steady herself.

'Leave the silly plate,' she said. His arm went around her waist as they began to straighten up. Next moment she was close to him, her head on his shoulder, and both his arms were tightly around her.

'Anna,' was all he could find to say. He ran glossy black locks of her hair through his fingers. She clung to him and she was still shaking with suppressed laughter.

He was piqued. He got his hand beneath her chin and lifted her face towards him. He kissed her brutally, then, almost fearfully, he let her go.

But she held on to him, held her face up to him again. He kissed her once more. Then she pulled away from him, jumbled things swiftly on to the tray, and left him gaping. The door closed behind her and he sank once more into his chair. He was a very puzzled man.

★ ★ ★

He had plenty of time for reflection that afternoon. It was getting late before anybody else came to see him. It was the one he had hoped to see but only half expected.

She entered the room slowly, drew up a chair and sat down in front of him. 'How are you feeling?' she said.

'I'm all right.'

Silence fell again. Jenkins burnt his fingers with the cigarette he had been smoking. That was the second time today. He flung the butt away from him with a silent curse.

He looked at the girl and said: 'I guess maybe I shouldn't have acted that way awhile back.'

'Do you think you shouldn't have?' she said. 'Are you sorry you did?'

His reply was vehement. 'No, by

Cracky, I ain't sorry.'

'That's all right then,' said the girl.

He reached out and caught hold of her hand. 'Do you really mean that, Anna?'

'I wouldn't have said it if I didn't.'

'Gosh, I've only known you a couple of days and I'm crazy about yuh. I hadn't hoped . . . ' He paused. He couldn't go on. He just gripped her hand tightly.

'They say men always fall for their nurses,' she said. 'It happens sometimes that the nurses fall for the men too. No matter how hard they try not to, no matter how cold and efficient they try to be . . . '

'Yeh,' said Jenkins. 'These things do happen.' He sounded almost miserable. He stopped but it was evident by his manner that he had something else on the tip of his tongue. The girl waited.

Finally he blurted out, 'Oh, why couldn't you have fallen for some handsome young cowboy with a share in a ranch an' money in the bank, instead of a hornery ol' troubleshooter like me.'

'Old? What do you mean — old?'

'I'm thirty-four.'

'You don't look a day above twenty-four.' When she first saw him Anna had thought him older than he was, but now, with a new animation in his face, battered and be-plastered though it was, and a softer light in his eyes, he looked like a merry youth.

'All right,' he said. 'I ain't so old — but I'm a badge-toter, a trouble-shooter.'

'Did you think you would always be a troubleshooter? Didn't you think that maybe some day you'd settle down and start being something else?'

'Wal — yes. I've always planned on having a little spread of my own someplace — a woman, maybe, and kids.' He stopped as if he'd bitten his tongue.

'Go on,' she said.

He went on. 'I wouldn't ask any woman to share my life with me until my job was finished.'

'But if a woman promised to wait?'

'I wouldn't want a woman to wait, wondering whether I was gonna be killed or not.'

'Women *will* wait, you know,' she said softly. 'Whether they're told to or not.'

Dusk was falling now and her face was shadowed by the dark smoke of her hair. Her eyes were faintly luminous. As if he could not bear to look at her any more he rose and crossed to the small window, looked out there as he spoke once more.

'I've got to go, Anna. There's lots of things I've got to do. Maybe when I've done 'em you will have changed your mind. Or maybe it won't be no use either way.'

She came up behind him. 'Don't say that, Thad,' she said.

He turned swiftly and caught hold of her. 'All right,' he said brutally. 'All right. I'm goin' now. I'll be back.'

He let her go. 'I'll be here,' she said as he crossed the room. The door closed behind him.

As she stayed behind in the dark room he crossed the stores, saying 'Adios' to her father, who said, 'Take care.'

He passed into the street, across it, up the alley beside Kavanaugh's place and through the back door. He found Sam in his little office. The saloonman did not seem surprised to see him.

Jenkins said: 'Did you find my gun-belt, Sam?'

'Yeh, it's up in your room — gun an' all.'

'Thanks,' said Jenkins. 'Tell me — is Red Porter in town tonight?'

'Yeh, he's in the bar. I tried to make him see he ain't wanted, but he's got a hide like an ol' bull-buffalo.'

'What's he like with a gun?'

'Purty fast. He fancies himself. Thad, are yuh aimin' to . . . '

'Yeh, Sam, I'm aimin' to. But don't worry, it won't be here . . . But it's gotta be.'

'There don't seem nothin' else for it,'

said Sam. 'An' if you didn't, I guess lots o' folks 'ud be kinda disappointed in yuh.'

'I'll go upstairs first,' said Jenkins and turned to leave.

'Thad . . . Hannibal's out front with Jigger Perks.'

'All right — I'll see 'em later.'

Jenkins went up the back-stairs and let himself into his room. He lit the lamp. His gun-belt with the old scarred walnut butt protruding from the holster, hung over the bedrail. The belt had been newly polished. Jenkins drew the gun. That had been finely oiled. He spun the chambers. They were full. He stood and weighed the gun in his hand, looking around the room like a man with a problem. Finally he put the gun back in the holster. He left the lamp burning as he went out of the room. He went along the landing to the top of the front stairs and looked over the balustrade to the saloon below. Then slowly he began to descend the stairs.

He was halfway down before he was

seen. The word passed around and finally what looked like a veritable sea of faces stared up at the tall, lean broad-shouldered man with the battered face and bandaged head.

Jenkins could see the grinning face of Red Porter among the mob but he chose to pretend he did not.

He stood stockstill on the stairs and called:

'Where's Red Porter? I'm lookin' for Red Porter.'

A murmur ran through the assembly. Then Red's bull-like voice bellowed: 'You ain't got to look any further, Jenkins! I'm right here!' The big redheaded man began to elbow his way to the foot of the stairs.

'You can stay right where you are, Porter,' said Jenkins. 'An' listen to what I've got to tell yuh . . . Stand still I say!'

His voice rang out authoritatively and despite himself Red stood stockstill.

'Hear me,' said Jenkins. 'Hear me everybody! Right now I'm callin' Red Porter a filthy, lying coward — I'm telling him to meet me at dawn tomorrow in the corral — in front of the blockhouse — or forever be branded as a yeller dog!'

The crowd murmured again, the voices swelling. Above them all rose Red's enraged bellow:

'You blabbermouthed skunk! I'll fix you right now!'

He drew his gun but his wrist was held. Other men grabbed hold of him. 'He's unarmed,' said one. 'You cain't shoot an unarmed man.'

Red struggled impotently, cursing Jenkins and everybody else. The cries of the crowd became threatening. The big man subsided, sheathed his gun.

'All right!' he shouted. 'I'll meet yuh in the corral at dawn. An' you'd better be armed this time.'

'I will be,' said Jenkins. He turned and went back up the stairs, back into his room.

He sat down in a chair there and felt suddenly deflated, tired. When some-body knocked on the door outside, however, he became alert. He drew his gun before he said, 'Come in.'

He tossed his gun on the bed as Hannibal Crocket entered, behind him another man, bigger, broader, shambling like an ape. Hannibal stepped aside to let him pass and Jenkins had a good look at him. His broad, curiously white face was that of a friendly child's and his blue eyes were guileless.

'This is Jigger Perks, Thad,' said Hannibal.

Jigger stuck out a hand as big as a soup plate. Jenkins took it and winced at its grip. 'Pleased to meet yuh, Jigger,' he said.

Jigger said: 'I seed you, Mr Jenkins. I seed you just now. I hope you whup Red Porter.'

'Thanks. I hope so too. Glad to know you're on my side.'

'Yep, I'm on your side, Mr Jenkins.' Jigger paused, his eyes wide. 'Gosh, Mr Jenkins, yore face is a mess.' A nine-year-old kid would have said it just the same way.

'Who done that to yore face, Mr Jenkins?'

'I guess lots o' folks are kinda responsible for my face,' said the other man with a twisted smile. 'Jigger, will you answer me a few questions?'

'Surely, Mr Jenkins.'

'The first one is: Do you remember Jack Kinsell?'

'Mr Crocket ast me that one,' said Jigger. 'Shore I remember Jack Kinsell.'

12

Night had fallen over the Sierra Madre. The sky was speckled with stars and there was a pale half-moon, like a slice of lemon in a julep. The peaks were etched against the sky. Darkness lay thickly in their hollows like treacle. The moon shone a little on the smooth walls of the pass, then the pockmarked shadows took over once more, higher up where the rocks soared to the stars.

On a shelf of rock, a deeper shade among many and as motionless as all of them, stood a man. He was erect and his arms were folded across his chest, his head bent a little as if he were brooding.

He was looking down into the darkness below and building pictures there. Such men as he shielded their faces from the stars, for they found no inspiration there.

Darkness was his solace and power. In darkness everything was right for him and there was no uncertainty. Here in this land spread out before him, which he could not see but could visualize all too clearly he had once been little more than a slave. It was ironical that to this place he had at last returned to bring off his final coup, the last of a long line. He was worth millions; for years he had told other men what to do, killed men who had withstood him because they reminded him of the implacable will of the father he had hated and because all the time, deep in his heart, he was frightened of being made a slave once more. Now there was nothing left of that: the full circle had been made. Nobody could stand in his way any more, power and riches were his forever . . .

Jack Kale chuckled softly, deeply, and the gentle echoes quivered around him. He lifted his head and spat outwards and down into the chasm below. Then he turned and looked back. Deep in the cave behind him a light glowed. It was a fire, but a man had to get very close to be able to see it and the smoke was drawn away above through a myriad tiny fissures in the rocks.

Jack Kale was walking towards that glow when the shot came, the sound of it echoing and re-echoing as if in a series of tunnels. He stood transfixed for a moment then he started forward and began to run.

His footsteps echoed from the hard floor and from up ahead came a babble of voices. Madness bubbled in Kale as he ran: what was happening now, who was being awkward and standing in his way? Then he turned the bend and stopped dead at the sight he saw in one raking glance.

The fire blazed in the centre and the men's heads were all turned away from it. Just within the fringes of its glow a crumpled figure lay on the floor — it looked more like a skimpy bag of bones than a man and the white, glassy-eyed face that stared upwards from some-where in the tattered bundle was the face of old Smoky.

A few yards away stood Slim with a smoking gun in his hand. He turned his head as Kale came into view. The gun swivelled too. The big blackclad man stood with his hands touching his belt. His face was pallid in the fire-glow, his eyes blazed.

'Don't get any ideas, Jack,' said Slim. 'Let me tell yuh what happened.'

'I don't want to hear what happened. I've told yuh . . . I've told yuh over an' over . . . There was no need f'r that . . . '

The voice was thick and trembling with rage. Kale seemed to be swelling as if he would burst any minute and explode across the cave in the direction of the thin-faced kid with the gun.

The gun did not waver. Slim said tonelessly: 'I gotta tell yuh. Smoky was lightin' his pipe. He dropped the burning stick on my hand, then, when I turned he went for his gun. He'd got it all worked out. He wasn't fast enough, that's all. There's his iron, right by him.' Slim pointed with his free hand.

'That's the way it happened, Jack,' said one of the men.

Kale did not seem to be listening. His eyes were fixed on Slim, his dark face was bloodless.

He said: 'You've never done as I told yuh. You've always thought you knew best. I told yuh not to do it — over an' over I told yuh. I bin good to you. I was fixin' to get rid o' Smoky later on — pension him off or somep'n an' make you my right-hand man . . . '

'It was him or me, Jack,' said Slim.

The big man went on as if the kid had not spoken. He seemed almost in a trance. His voice was soulful as he said:

'You shouldn't've done it, Slim. Not when I told yuh not to. Yuh can't go on like that — you're finished, Slim. Finished.' Kale paused. Then he said softly to no one in particular. 'Take his gun.'

Slim backed till he reached the wall

of the cave. There was a little red spot on each of his pale cheeks. His queer deepset eyes were glowing and that little twisted smile was on his lips.

'*Take his gun,*' he sneered. 'Just like that. I'll kill the first man who moves.'

He began to work his way slowly along the wall; his gun shifted slightly in a slow arc. His eyes shifted with it. He drew level with Kale.

'Get over there with the others, Jack,' he said. 'Turn around — walk in front of me. Keep your hands away from them guns.'

'Don't be a fool, Slim,' chanted the big man.

'A fool! That's rich. Must I hand my iron over to you an' let you shoot me with it? Move!'

Kale began to walk forward. Slim stepped behind him and whisked one of his guns from its holster.

'Now I've got two instead o' just one,' he said. 'Twelve slugs. An' I can shoot faster than any of yuh . . . That's far enough, Jack. Turn around.'

Slowly Kale turned. His rage had left him. He was relaxed. One hand still hung near the gun Slim had left him.

'Go for it, Jack,' the kid taunted him. 'What's the matter — scared? Go on — go for it! . . . No? All right then, just elevate your paws.'

Kale moved a little further back and slowly began to raise his hands. Behind him, almost hidden by him, scarfaced Benny went for his gun.

Slim laughed and his left-hand gun blazed. Benny gave a choking cry and pitched forward, knocking against Kale's shoulder. As Kale staggered his hand dipped and rose.

In the cave the rolling echoes of shots made the night hideous. The firelight was obscured by blue powdersmoke.

★　★　★

Dawn etched the peaks of the Sierra Madre in a bluey-grey setting. It drifted like smoke down the main drag of Jonestown, turning slowly into a pearly

185

haze. High in the sky the glow spread as if the sun was already trying to break through to greet the morning, to help bring a gentle peaceful sunkissed morning.

Jonestown was an unusual sight for so early. Men were already appearing on the street, drifting down it in twos and threes and in groups, keeping to the sidewalks most of them, moving towards the old blockhouse then drifting away and vanishing like the mist.

But still others entered the street in their places, followed in their wake. Not all of them managed to dissolve like the mist and pretty soon the vicinity of the blockhouse was ringed by furtive heads, like gophers peeping out of their holes. There was menace in the air, subtle but evident. The situation would have seemed funny were it not so tragic on a morning like this.

Still the men kept coming and many now, bolder than others, began to take their stand around the corral-fence.

And there were horsemen riding into town now, tying their mounts to hitching-racks and joining this rapidly-swelling rank.

The riders became more numerous and the men at the corral craned their necks to identify them, and greeted them as they approached.

People who lived within good view of the corral stood at their doors and windows and waited. Right opposite the old blockhouse which dominated the scene, a throwback from even bloodier times, Lye Mowbray stood on his doorstep in his white apron. At his side was a sawn-off shotgun. Lye did not trust anybody. And he took no chances.

At a window above him his daughter sat, her hair a dark stream around her shoulders, her face, framed by it, white in the morning light. Her eyes were wide with anxiety, a little red-rimmed with sleeplessness. Yet Lye when he greeted her that morning thought she had never looked so lovely. She reminded him poignantly of his dead wife.

On a morning such as this it was perhaps meet that he should think back to his own younger, faster times. He had been a riproaring hellion when he had won the love of Ella Sanders, the beauty of Rincon, New Mexico. He had money saved. Some of it not gotten by fair means either — though that was another story. The land back there was being grabbed right and left by richer, more powerful men. He tried to fight them and lost, so he and Ella and their six months old baby, Anna, moved. They wandered a lot before they discovered the mushroom pile which was called Jonestown and, because there was something about the unrelenting hardness of the place which put Lye on his mettle, he decided he'd settle there. Ella, as usual, was obedient to his wishes. He built his store and had merchandize hauled from Nogales and Tucson. Things were very hard at first. Then, because they were the only all-purpose store in the territory, because they were friendly people who did not dun their customers — though Lye was a nasty customer if he was crossed — they prospered.

Then Ella died and, within the space of a few short months Lye Mowbray changed from a still-young go-ahead man to a lethargic old one. Yet, despite him now, his store continued to prosper, brightened more and more by the presence of his growing daughter, probably the only person who could make him smile.

He made money fast. He could have moved and sought fresher, kinder fields. But he had no wish to do so now. He had gotten to understand the people of Jonestown, many of them hard and bitter like himself.

His daughter had a yen for nursing: he sent her to Tucson for proper training. When she went she seemed to him still little more than a child. He missed her terribly. She visited him from time to time and he began to notice the subtle change in her. Then she returned for good. And she was a woman.

She took him in hand and under her influence he began to mellow and become a rational being — after the years of bitterness and useless grief. Since then she had been his guiding light at all times and he worshipped her as he had worshipped her mother.

Last night she had come into his room and blown out the lamp, asking him to sit with her in the dark and talk like they had done when she was a child and her mother had been alive. He had an idea what she wanted to tell him. His surmises had been correct.

As he stood at the doorway, knowing that she was above him, waiting and hoping, praying maybe, he was savage because he could not help her. It was inevitable that some of his rage should be directed at the man she loved — because that man was so very much like he had been himself when he was younger. Fearless, pigheaded, hard, ruthless. He had brought his bride to this harsh place — although in his heart he had known she hated it — and she had died. He blamed himself — he had killed her.

He did not want anything like that to happen to his daughter, moulded in her mother's image, loving greatly as she had done. Yet, even in his jealousy, he knew that the tall broad-shouldered stranger was worthy of her love . . .

Standing in his doorway, his shotgun by his side, Lye Mowbray was a prey to conflicting emotions. Even in his bitterness and his misery he had always tried to be a just man. Since then he had found tolerance too. Here was the supreme test for that tolerance. His mind was in a turmoil, a nightmare reverie.

His reverie was broken suddenly by a shout, a louder buzz from the men at the corral. He looked up. Red Porter had arrived.

The big fellow stood in the middle of the corral now. He had taken off his hat and thrown it in the dust like a gauntlet before him. The morning light glittered in his mane of red hair.

He threw back his head and bellowed, 'Where is he?'

Nobody answered him.

13

A man walked casually past Lye Mowbray, watching Red, not seeming to notice Lye there in the doorway. It was Red's pard, the shifty vindictive-looking Cal. He walked away from the corral and leaned against a hitching-rack with his thumbs in his belt and still watched Red.

Lye Mowbray watched Red too and, standing in the doorway, his face impassive in the morning light, he made his decision.

The big man was still bawling. 'Where is he? Where is the yeller rat? I told yuh he was a no-good. What's his game?' He was working himself up into another of his famous furies.

'He never intended to come. He's got us all waitin' around here for some purpose. You mark my words. You ought to've let me finish him off last night.'

Men began to look at each other uncertainly as Red's words struck home and he, believing himself now, bawled at them again. Standing there with his legs spread apart, his leonine head thrown back while the morning light etched his Herculean figure with growing clearness, he was a commanding figure, easy for men who had gotten up in the early morning to wait tensely for something to happen, to believe.

A murmur ran through the ranks. Men began to argue. Red became silent and stood like a stolid figure of power and wrath and triumph as he looked down the empty street. A figure appeared suddenly from Kavanaugh's place and a sudden hush fell.

Then, as the figure got nearer, there was a snarl from the crowd. It was only Sam, the saloonkeeper. He walked slowly towards the corral. He did not change his direction until he was almost upon the big man then, as he did so, he said:

'You'd better say your prayers, Red. He's comin'.'

The big man laughed harshly. His chest swelled. He was confidence incarnate. A ripple ran through the crowd as the word was passed along. Then the hush fell, more portentous than ever, as another figure came slowly from Kavanaugh's Bar, strode to the middle of the street and began to advance.

Thaddeus Jenkins came on slowly, with a slight limp. His hands brushed his sides. He looked straight in front of him. He did not pause in his stride when a man came out of a doorway across the street.

The man called softly, 'Jenkins. Jenkins.'

Jenkins stopped on one foot, twisted; he was a blur of motion as he half-faced Red's pard, Henny. A single shot echoed down the street; something like a prairie puff-ball blossomed for a moment at Jenkins' hip. Henny's gun was out of its holster but it remained by his side as he slowly crumpled on the sidewalk. The gun slid along the boards to drop in the dust beneath. Henny lay still.

There was a shade of sadness in Jenkins' eyes as he came on. Red did not deserve that such a man should die for him: a man who had given fair warning, had been a squareshooter.

In the distance the rising sun was etching the peaks of the mountains with a rosy light. The light crept across the sand and the sparse grass, along the trail to the main street of Jonestown. A street which seemed suddenly wide to the people who lined it near the corral and clustered against the fences and the old blockhouse and the stores and the log-cabins and the clapboard and iron-sheeting shacks. The street was long and wide and the man who strode down it a pygmy, but swelling as he came on and the light shone on him and the sun made a halo for his bandaged head.

He began to change direction and for

the first time his eyes sought the corral and the man who stood alone in the centre of it, all those people around him, but still alone, a big figure.

Jenkins saw the face of Red Porter, set in a grin now in which there was maybe just a hint of strain, now there was no more shouting, no more laughter, only the silence and the scuff of a man's feet advancing slowly in the dust.

Then there was the slap-slap of other feet, swiftly moving, and somebody shouted as a man, gun drawn, dropped from the sidewalk in Jenkins' path.

A single shot boomed, the echoes rolling up the slopes of the trail. Red's pard, Cal, stood transfixed, a terrible look of surprise on his face. Then his gun slid from his lax hand and hit the ground and he pitched forward on top of it. Jenkins' hand remained on the butt of the gun in his holster. His eyes shifted, caught those of Lye Mowbray, standing in the doorway of his stores with the smoking shotgun in his hands.

Neither of them said anything. They understood each other.

Jenkins, who had paused for only a second, began to walk again. He passed through the wide corral-gate and his eyes were on Red Porter's face now, red, swelling as he got nearer. His eyes watched Red Porter's eyes and he knew he was going to kill the big man. Knew it as surely as he had known Henny had died in the dust behind him and Cal too; and he remembered the light in Lye Mowbray's eyes, and the glimpse he had had of the face in the window above, brave and waiting; and he knew he would kill Red Porter as sure as the sun was warm on his wounded head, and there was life in himself and a strange sadness struggling there too.

He saw the choleric eyes of Red Porter widen but he did not pause in his stride and his hand moved smoothly and swiftly. He felt the gun buck in his hand, twice, heard the reports like a single crash in his ears. There was a whiff of powdersmoke in his nostrils and he saw the little puffs of dust blossom from the broad red shirt-front before him and he saw those choleric eyes, wider now than seemed possible, just once more as Red staggered towards him.

He did not stop walking until he stood over the man who lay face downwards in the dust and knew he was dead. He heard the long-drawn murmuring breath like a single sigh, from the crowd and he came to himself, looking around him, feeling the soft breeze on his face, the sun on his head, knowing he was alive and whole, and turning and walking away from the staring faces.

He shook Lye Mowbray's hand then went past him into the soft gloom of the stores where Anna awaited him. She came to him slowly and put her arms around him and her head on his breast and, for a moment, neither of them said anything.

He spoke first as he gently pushed her away from him.

'Stay here, Anna,' he said. 'I've got to go now. There are folks waiting for me.'

She stood in the gloom, shapely in her long gown, and watched him go. He did not look back and he passed her father and went on into the street.

Outside Hannibal Crocket came to meet him. He was mounted and led Jenkins' horse. Behind him on a rawboned grey mare rode Jigger Perks.

He grinned. 'I told yuh you'd whup him, Mr Jenkins,' he said.

Jenkins mounted and the three of them rode out of town, leaving behind them the buzzing crowd in the corral, the body they surrounded, the smaller groups around the two bodies in the street.

Jenkins' face was impassive and grim. That task was finished now. There was other work to be done, much work before he could finish, before he could return and claim his reward and his peace.

★　★　★

200

The three men veered off the trail before they reached the mine. They made a wide detour, following a tortuous trail of their own through the arid fantastic wastes of the badlands.

By just past noon they were at the boulder-strewn foothills behind the Sierra Madre completely hidden from sight of the town and the mine. They might have been wanderers in a strange uninhabited land, cut off from all sight and sound of human kind, or even beasts or flying things.

It was a land of cruel majestic beauty: the peaks soaring up above them, the rocks tinted by the sun into graduating shades of rainbow colouring and, behind them, until the purple heat-haze obscured the horizon, a yellow waste with fantastically twisted coloured vegetation and huge boulders, lying as if tossed there carelessly by a giant hand.

Against one of these boulders, on the slopes of the foothills, the three men sat in the shade and had a meal. Biscuits and dried fruit, and cold coffee from a water-bottle because they did not wish to light a fire.

'Do you know where you are now, Jigger?' said Thaddeus Jenkins.

The big simple man answered boastfully through a mouthful of food. 'Shore I know where I am. I know all this territory. Nobody knows this territory like I do.'

'He's right, Thad,' said Hannibal Crocket. 'He's done some ridin' around this countryside in his day. Once we thought he'd gone for good, he was away a whole week. But he came back, as large as life — just a little thirsty that's all. Any other man would have been buzzard-bait. Jigger must have the constitution of a camel.'

'Where did you go that time you got lost, Jigger?' said Jenkins.

'I found me a li'l ol' cave nobody else knows about an' I set up there an' laughed at 'em all. They didn't know I was up there — they thought the buzzards had got me.' Jigger swelled his great chest. He had a subhuman expansion. 'But the buzzards don't hurt me.'

Hannibal said: 'Folks in town had been joshing him I guess. He feels it sometimes. Then he goes an' hides himself . . . '

Jigger went on as if the thin man had not spoken. 'I set up there an' laughed at 'em all,' he repeated.

'Many a man wishes he could do that,' said Jenkins gently. 'Will you show me an' Hannibal that cave o' yours — that cave nobody else knows about — an' all the other caves you know.'

'Wal,' said Jigger. His brow became puckered. The two men watched him.

Hannibal said: 'You promised to bring Mr Jenkins out an' show him all the territory.'

Jigger's face suddenly broke into a huge grin. 'Yes,' he said. 'I did. Mr Jenkins whupped Red Porter. I'll show him all the territory an' my caves an' things — all my caves an' things.'

Beside the big simple man Jenkins blew out an audible sigh of relief.

'You're plenty *muy amigo*, Jigger,' he said.

He took out his pack of cigarettes and passed them around. All three men lit up and smoked gratefully and in silence. There was a proud little smile on Jigger Perks' face.

A few minutes later they threw their cigarette-stubs away, watching them sink into the soft treacherous sand, and bestirred themselves. They mounted their horses and began to forge up the slope.

'This leads into the back-end of the pass,' said Hannibal.

'Yeh, that's it,' said Jigger. He looked a little aggrieved. *He* was the guide.

Hannibal said no more but let the big man pass him and forge a little way ahead. A little later they dismounted and began to lead their horses, Jigger turning every now and then to wave them on. Then, quite suddenly, he vanished.

The two men halted. 'Now where has the crazy coot gone?' said Hannibal.

Jenkins pointed. 'He went in between them two big rocks.'

The two men started off again. Leading their horses they passed between the two huge boulders. A sound made them turn, their hands instinctively flying to their guns. Jigger Perks appeared, cackling like a naughty child. He beckoned with a forefinger then vanished again around a sharp corner. They went around a towering razor-edge of rock into a narrow cleft in the rock-walls. They turned a bend and Jigger and his horse was in front of them and, looking up they could see, high above, a narrow strip of blue sky. Jigger turned and beckoned gleefully.

They caught up with him and followed him along the smooth floor of the cleft, the walls so close each side of them at times, that their horses, snorting fearfully, had to be cajoled past them. Jigger's mount, which was the biggest of the three, and which almost got stuck a few times, did not show any signs of fear. He was evidently well-used to this journey.

Finally the cleft widened a little and Jigger hastened his pace. Before them the two men saw a wider patch of blue sky, the peaks etched against it. Then they came out into the open and Jigger was pointing downwards.

'The pass,' he said. 'The pass.'

The two men stood on a terrifying lip of rock and looked down.

'Yell, that's the pass awlright,' said Hannibal. 'The back end too. I guess we're in Mexico now, uh?'

Jigger nodded his head. 'Yep, we're in Mexico.'

'How do we get off here?' said Jenkins. 'It's making me dizzy.'

Jigger grinned and turned, leading the way once more. He climbed onto his mount.

'Hosses slide here if yuh don't hold 'em,' he said.

The other two men followed his example. Up in the saddle Thaddeus Jenkins turned and looked down the dizzy heights. He shuddered.

'Gosh, I hope Jigger ain't forgotten his way,' he said. 'One false step and we're piecemeal.'

The big man led them along the edge of the precipice for a couple of hundred yards or so and then veered away. There was a collective sigh of relief from the other two. While they were drawing breath Jigger vanished again.

'Hey!' said Hannibal Crocket and urged his horse forward.

Clattering and sliding, Jenkins' mount followed. 'Easy,' yelled Hannibal as his companion nearly cannoned into him. He was poised on the top of a slope, a bumpy, tortuous boulder-strewn declivity which reached down to the floor of the pass below.

Jigger was already well on his way, his mare almost sliding on her rump. He turned and grinned at the two men and waved them on.

'Wal, if a loopy cuss like him kin do it I guess we can,' said Hannibal. He sounded a little doubtful however.

'It ain't him who's doin' it, it's his hoss,' said Jenkins. 'She must've bin crossed with a mountain-goat.' He shrugged his broad shoulders. 'Ah, well — maybe Red was the luckiest after all.' He urged his unwilling mount down the slope.

He could hear Hannibal sliding behind him. His own horse seemed to be going with the speed of a racing stallion and the shale clattered beneath his hoofs. Jenkins realized that the beast just couldn't stop himself. He leaned far back in the saddle and threw his weight on the taut reins.

The horse's speed slackened a little; he missed craggy outcrops of rock by a hairsbreadth, and Jenkins was almost lying back on his rump. The terrifying motion stopped suddenly; the horse stood still, snorting, its flanks heaving. They were on the floor of the pass. Jenkins could hardly believe it; he looked upwards, then he urged his horse forward out of the path of Hannibal Crocket's headlong flight.

By a superhuman effort the thin man hauled in his mount, gentled him with his hand and soothing words. Jigger, who had landed-up a bit further down, came up to them.

'The pass,' he said with the air of a magician saying 'hey presto.'

Jenkins and Crocket looked at each other. 'The pass!' they echoed feelingly.

Jigger grinned, dismounted from his horse and began to wend his way up the other side. With gestures of weary resignation the other two followed him.

When he vanished again up there a few minutes later they almost expected him to reappear once more in a puff of smoke. But he only hollered to them out of the depths of a cave.

They went into the dim interior. There was straw in a corner, an upturned packing-case, a few cooking utensils. 'I set up here an' I laughed at 'em all,' said Jigger.

'Pardner, you had reason to,' said Thaddeus Jenkins with deep feeling.

Jigger led them out. 'I know of

another one,' he said. 'A great big one. Up there.' He pointed to where the peaks soared to the glittering blue-steel of the sky.

Jenkins and Crocket exchanged glances. 'Lead on,' said Jenkins.

'We'll have to leave the hosses in my cave if we go this way,' said Jigger. 'The only way for hosses is right around the other side — when yuh come in from the other end of the pass.'

He showed them the huge hook he had stolen from the blacksmith's shop in Jonestown and driven into the wall of the cave. To it they tethered their horses. Then they began to climb.

They were silent. Jenkins' thoughts were rather peevish. What was he doing scrambling about the Sierra Madre like a mountain-goat? Did he expect to find anything like this? Was not this a ludicrous anti-climax after his victory over Red Porter that morning? All day so far the only signs of life (if they could be called 'signs of life') they had seen were the bleached bones of a horse.

He was irritated when Jigger, who as usual was forging in front, stopped and threw his head back. As he got nearer to the simple man he realized he was sniffing like a hound-dog who had gotten a scent of something.

'I smell smoke,' said Jigger.

'F'r Pete's sake,' said Jenkins. 'I don't smell nothin'. I'm all dried up. Do you smell anythin', Hannibal?'

'Nope,' said Hannibal.

'Smoke,' said Jigger again, unheeding. Half-crouching he forged ahead again.

When they caught up with him he was on his belly between two rocks.

'Look,' he said.

They followed the direction of his stabbing finger and from a narrow crack in the rocks just in front of his nose saw a wisp of blue smoke lazily curling.

'Smoke from fires. Big cave underneath,' said Jigger rapidly, his blue eyes shining.

He crawled further to another larger

crack. He lay down on his side and applied his ear to it.

He looked up. 'Many men down there,' he said. He held up both his hands, the fingers spread. 'More men than that down there.'

They got down beside him. He beckoned, then crawled again and they followed. He put his finger to his lips.

They looked over the edge of a lip of rock. 'We're over top of the mouth of the cave,' whispered Jigger.

Two men were sitting on a boulder out there. One of them rose, his back to the watchers. His figure was so familiar that Thaddeus Jenkins felt suddenly breathless, as if a hand had gotten hold of his heart and squeezed it.

14

Silence lay over the cluster of shacks at the base of the Devil's Fingers. There had been no mining that day; there would not be any done there anymore. The mine was closing down and the personnel was moving to a place in New Mexico where the firm's prospectors had made another strike.

Nobody would be sorry to leave this hell-hole after the months of toil, and unfriendliness, and frustration as the gold slowly petered out. And on top of it all now was tragedy and sorrow.

Men leaned against the bar in the canteen and drank almost in silence. The piano was covered by a green cloth, and nobody went near it.

Up the slopes behind the canteen another bunch of men were gathered around a cluster of pitiful mounds. By the light of a lantern, swinging in the hand of an oldtimer, they were placing boards and crosses at the heads of these mounds and propping them up with small boulders, covering the mounds with other rocks so that no prowling creatures of the night could disturb them.

They were like men in a dream, for they did not know what to do next; this pitiless country was alien to most of them; they were aware that somebody should pay for this crime but they did not know who — or where to find them.

There were rumours that a lawman was already here on the trail of the gang, a stranger whom the townsfolk had reviled, as they reviled all strangers, but were now willing to help. The miners and railwaymen, however, had little faith in the people of Jonestown.

There were rumours also that a batch of lawmen were coming from Tucson, as well as the company's own private investigator from back East. What could a fancy private detective do in a wild untamed country like this against people who were human wolves? What could any lawman do for that matter: the bandits were probably deep in some hideyhole miles the other side of the border by now!

They might even have gone in the other direction. There were so many places they could go in this vast arid territory. The men finished their task and, each with his own similar thoughts, turned to descend the slopes. From somewhere in the shadows behind a hoarse voice hailed them.

They turned again, alert, swinging pickaxes and sledges in their hands. Those of them who had guns reached for them. The voice said: 'We come in peace, boys,' and two figures loomed out of the darkness.

The oldtimer with the lantern swung it high. 'It's two o' them town jaspers,' he said. 'What are they doin' here?'

The two men came on. The one in front was thin to the point of emaciation, his cheeks hollow, his eyes sunken in the light. By contrast the other one was a giant — shambling out of a dream in the dusk over the graves of murdered men.

'Some of you men know me,' said the first one. 'Hannibal Crocket is my name. I've never done any of yuh any harm. This is a friend o' mine, Jigger Perks. Jigger knows more about these mountains than any other man living, and he's discovered the hideout of the train-bandits.'

The mineworkers moved nearer, giving themselves time to let the Jonestown man's words sink in. Then one of them said:

'He's tryin' to be funny.'

Hannibal's voice rang out again. 'You damn fools! You're wasting time. There's a man up there watching the hideout — the marshal who tailed that gang all the way from Texas — if they catch him he'll be dead meat pronto. Look alive, get your hosses an' follow us.'

His vehemence was very convincing — some turned and ran down the hill shouting, but others still hovered, mistrustful.

'Where's Rippon?' yelled somebody. 'Rippon.'

From down below in the canteen there were answering cries. A broad beam of light suddenly slashed out across the ground as a door was flung wide.

'What's goin' on?' bellowed a voice.

Running men ran across the beam of light, joining those who were running down the hill.

Hannibal and Jigger fetched their horses and descended the slope themselves, almost driving the disbelieving ones before them.

A stocky figure came to meet them. 'What's this?' said Rippon.

'We want help an' we want it quickly,' said Hannibal. 'I don't want to waste any more time talking. Every man jack of you get a hoss an' follow us if you want to catch the men who murdered your pardners and stole your payroll.'

Rippon did not hesitate. He knew Crocket a little personally, and more by reputation. He bawled:

'Hosses, everybody! Look lively, you swabs, this is what we've been waiting for.'

Barely ten minutes later he and Hannibal, together with the delighted Jigger, were at the head of a bunch of about two dozen men.

'Come on,' said Hannibal. 'And make no more noise than you can help. Sound travels a long way in these mountains.'

* * *

The man lying on his stomach on the lip of rock, in the shelter now of a saw-toothed boulder, watched the light slowly fade behind the peaks. It was pearly and then, suddenly, it was a dark velvet grey as total night fell swiftly, as it did in that part of the West. Pale specks of stars began to wink, giving a shadowy diffused projection of the peaks. But there was no moon.

The man had watched people pass in and out of the cave. The familiar figure he had seen two or three times.

Now they were all inside there and he could see nothing. But the scent of woodsmoke was in his nostrils and he could hear a soft humming, like a hive of bees deep in the ground.

The night had fallen cold after the heat of the day. Another trick of this God-forsaken corner of the old US. He was beginning to get chilly and stiff and, because the ground around him was peppered with loose rocks which he could not now see, he was scared to move in case he made a noise.

This waiting irked him. A chill breeze brought pain to his wounded face and nervous tension made his bandaged head feel as big as two. He had done enough hanging around — far too much in fact! He wanted action! What had happened to Hannibal and Jigger? It seemed ages since they went! Had they ever reached the mine? And what had happened if they had?

The buzzing from down below was becoming louder. It sounded like some kind of an altercation was going on. He figured that, with the racket they were making, they would not be able to hear him if he moved. Even so he paused. Maybe any sound up here would echo underneath.

Dare he take that chance? Or must he keep on waiting for the arrival of the others? It seemed to him at that moment, so cramped and wretched was he, that the others would never come.

Down below the voices quietened again and he cursed himself for not acting when he had the chance.

Suddenly somebody started to sing. It was an eerie whining sound coming from the bowels of the earth. Then he thought somebody shouted. The singing died. The murmuring of voices got louder again. The man in the darkness above fervently wished he could hear what was being said.

He rose slowly to his knees, flexing his arms, then rubbing his hands down his stiff cold body. Down below there were just vague shapes; he could see the boulder where two of the men had sat during the daylight, but nothing moved there now.

He placed both his hands on the rock in front of him and levered himself to his feet, slowly and with painful concentration. He began to move sideways carefully, straining his eyes in the meagre light of the stars, fearful of tumbling over the edge of giving the alarm in any other way. If he were caught now he would be killed and the bandits would run like foxes — probably never to be caught. He did not underrate the daring and cleverness of that gang and their leader.

He began to descend a slope, stopping every now and then to listen. Finally he reached a small flat piece of tableland. To his right a hump of rock rose before him. The buzzing of voices became a little clearer. He realized he was in a flatbottomed hollow somewhere at the back of the cave. He decided it must be a mighty big one — and with some hellish twists in it.

He forged on a little further and began to climb again. Maybe he could get to a position where he would be able to see more of the cave-mouth. He was pretty reckless now.

Suddenly he froze. The voices were much louder. He could hear the stamping of horses' hoofs too and the chinking of bridles. He threw himself flat and began to wriggle along laboriously on his stomach.

He peered around a boulder and saw the clearing below him, much nearer now, and the black patch that was the mouth of the cave.

As he watched a glow began to steadily illuminate this patch. It got brighter and finally he saw the figure of a man holding a lantern which shone on the metal bridles of horses; on the gunbelts and spurs of other men, as they came out of the darkness behind.

He saw a man advance with a saddle and place it on a horse's back. All was bustle. He heard a man curse, another one laugh, another one say, 'I shore have had my bellyful of this goldarned cave.'

Then a voice that Jenkins recognized said: 'Hurry it up back there. Yuh want to go don't yuh? Awlright then — let's get goin'.'

Jenkins became tense, his brain in a sudden turmoil. That was a smack in the eye surely — Hannibal, where the hell are you?

He drew back as the first men led their horses out of the cave. The lantern bobbed nearer.

'Douse that light now, damn you!' snarled the wellknown voice. 'Or do you want we should light a bonfire out there and let everybody know we're here plumb all the way to Texas.'

Another voice grumbled inaudibly and the lantern went out.

Now Jenkins could only see vague moving shapes in the gloom, could hear the slow scraping of hoofs, the creak of leather, the chink of steel. Pretty soon he figured the whole bunch must be out on the clearing before the cave.

He knew then what he must do.

He took his gun from its holster and checked it quickly. He ran his other hand along his belt to ascertain that he had his full quota of cartridges.

He heard the well-known voice say:

'All right then, let's get movin'.'

But he could not see its owner.

He picked out the two men nearest him and told himself they were coldblooded killers who deserved to be shot down like dogs. His number was up anyway he guessed, he might as well take as many as he could with him; in that exalted moment he felt no regrets about anything, no fear about what was to come. He fanned the hammer of his gun and it bucked and sang. Its music was sweet in his ears and the powdersmoke was like the smell of rare wine.

He saw the two men go down, heard

another one yell out, a horse scream shrilly. Then the bunch were fanning out, moving into the shadows. He saw flashes in all directions and ducked down behind a rock as bullets whined around him or ricochetted into the night.

The echoes of the gunfire rolled among the peaks and the night was like morning with the light of the gun flashes. Then the echoes died again and there was silence except for the murmur of voices. Jenkins strained his ears but he could not hear what was being said. He could not see anything either except the three still shadows on the floor of the clearing. It pleased him that he had got three of them instead of only two.

He heard movements, stealthy ones; the rattle of stones. They stopped. He lay flat and stuck his gun around the corner of the rock. He wondered if his head, with its white bandages, was a good target. He kept it low. He waited, straining his eyes.

The sounds came again and he thought he saw a movement too. He fired. He heard a shot then the night exploded again. He drew back into cover. There was something wet on his left arm. He ran his fingers experimentally across the place then cursed in surprise. He had been slightly winged!

He wormed his way along to the other end of the boulder. The firing was more desultory now. He could hear the bullets smacking into the rock or whining away into the night.

There was a chorus of echoes, swelling and dying, then swelling again.

There was something aimless about that shooting and, old gunfighter that he was, he realized its portent. A bunch of them down there were keeping him occupied, keeping him in cover, while under cloak of the din others were moving to get on his flanks. He turned around, sat with his back to the rock and began to reload his gun. He was perfectly cool now. Let the skunks come — he'd give 'em a run for their money!

He muttered a curse and gave a slight shrug. That relieved his feelings a bit. He decided he had been a sap to think he would ever settle down and die with his boots on. In these last couple of days he had been as happy, he figured, as any man of his calibre had a right to be. Anna would forget him. She would find some nice clean young cowboy who would suit her better. That was the way it ought to be, so who was he to whine?

He picked up a stone idly and tossed it a little way to the left of him. A gun flashed. He fired at the flash and grinned wolfishly as he heard an answering cry of pain. He opened his mouth wide and let out a piercing yell. The Rebel yell that had struck terror into the hearts of many men. He flattened himself against the rock as the bullets came thick and fast. He calculated the position of those men nearest to him.

There was a lull and spacing his shots, moving his gun between each one, he began triggering again.

The night was hideous then; he felt slugs pluck at his clothes, a sharp pain in his thigh; and the echoes were swelling to almost deafen him.

Another cry, similar to his own Rebel yell, was ringing in his ears and somebody was laughing insanely. It seemed like he was going mad. There were men all around him and, as he lifted his gun once more, a familiar voice called his name.

'Hannibal,' he called. 'Here.' But he realized that Hannibal could not reach him without running a gauntlet of fire.

Everything was drowned for him then as the firing began once more with redoubled fury. He looked down into the clearing. Everything was taken out of his hands now and he felt suddenly weak and helpless. He put his hand to his thigh and it came away wet and sticky.

He leaned back against the rock and reloaded his gun once more, and then, looking up he saw the figure moving to the right of him. He threw himself flat as a gun flamed. He felt the slug pluck at the bandages on his head. Then, flat on his stomach with his gun held out in front of him, he was retaliating.

The figure began to move, climbing up the rocks. There was something very familiar about it. Jenkins fired and knew he had missed. He realized his hand was shaking. He gritted his teeth. He rose to his feet and, limping, began to follow.

'It's no use, Slim,' he called. 'You'd better stay where you are.'

At the sound of the voice the other man stiffened. For a moment of time he remained suspended there. Then he moved swiftly.

Jenkins threw himself sideways, firing savagely, seeing the man etched there by the gun-flashes, feeling the slugs whistle around him. There was something clutching at his throat, almost choking him, as he watched the man fall. He walked slowly into the gloom and found him lying there flat on his back his face turned upwards, shining dully in the light from the stars.

The eyes were open, there was a queer little smile on the face. The lips moved slowly.

'It's you, Thad.'

'Yes, it's me, Slim.'

'I never figured you'd catch up with us or I'd've started movin' afore now.'

'Where's Jack Kale, Slim?'

The other's voice was weaker, more halting, as he answered. 'We had a fight — I killed him — an' took over the leadership — o' the gang . . . You'll find his body in a split in the rocks — somewhere along the back here — there's two more bodies with it.' Slim's lips jerked at the corners, something like a chuckle escaped from them. 'Jack's got the place of honour — like he's allus wanted it . . . We — we put his body on top . . . '

Light footfalls sounded behind Jenkins. He turned swiftly.

'It's me, Thad,' said Hannibal Crocket. As the thin man joined him Jenkins turned once more to the dying man.

Slim's hand was clawing at his side. His eyes were suddenly unnaturally wide. Jenkins caught hold of the hand.

'Rest easy, Slim.'

Slim's eyes became fixed. 'Adios, Thad,' he whispered huskily.

He closed his eyes. The queer little smile was still on his face.

Jenkins rose to his feet, dusting off his knees.

Hannibal Crocket said: 'You knew the younker, Thad?'

Jenkins did not look at him. He said tonelessly, 'He was my half brother. His mother was my mother. She was a good woman but when my father died she went kinda haywire. She hitched-up with a no-good. He left her when she was having a child. Slim was that child. I guess he inherited most of the bad traits of his father . . . But he had his mother's guts!'

Jenkins voice died. He looked down at the bundle at his feet. Then he said:

'I guess this is what I was meant to

do before I hung up my guns.'

Hannibal said: 'Come away, Thad. I'll send a couple of the boys up to take care of him.'

The two men descended the slope to the clearing, where sullen bandits were being roped in a long line. Hannibal spoke to a few of the men. Jenkins did not speak to anybody. He followed his friend. They were riding slowly down the pass before Hannibal ventured to talk.

He said: 'Did yuh hear Jigger laugh? He put the fear o' death into 'em. But he showed himself and the skunks got him.'

'Pore Jigger,' said Jenkins and they fell silent again.

They were moving across flat sand and a faint glow in the sky before them was the reflection of the lights of Jonestown when one of them spoke again.

Jenkins said: 'Time to hang up my law-guns I guess. I plumb near took 'em to the Happy Huntin' Grounds with me this time. Time I settled down, got a little spread o' my own, a woman, kids maybe.'

'You've got the woman I guess,' said his pardner. 'All you want now is the land.'

'I guess there's a few spare chunks around here, uh?'

'I guess so. But it's mighty hard country.'

'I've suddenly taken a helluva likin' to it.'

'In that case I guess a hornery troubleshooter like you won't have any difficulty in taming himself a chunk of it.'

The lights of Jonestown blossomed more brightly. They were just a glow in a rather sordid waste but to one weary troubleshooter as he urged his horse to a gallop, they were a promise of rest and peace and happiness.

We do hope that you have enjoyed reading this large print book.

Did you know that all of our titles are available for purchase?

We publish a wide range of high quality large print books including:
Romances, Mysteries, Classics
General Fiction
Non Fiction and Westerns

Special interest titles available in large print are:
The Little Oxford Dictionary
Music Book, Song Book
Hymn Book, Service Book

Also available from us courtesy of Oxford University Press:
Young Readers' Dictionary
(large print edition)
Young Readers' Thesaurus
(large print edition)

For further information or a free brochure, please contact us at:
Ulverscroft Large Print Books Ltd.,
The Green, Bradgate Road, Anstey,
Leicester, LE7 7FU, England.
Tel: (00 44) **0116 236 4325**
Fax: (00 44) **0116 234 0205**

RODEO RENEGADE

Ty Kirwan

When English couple Rufus and Nancy Medford inherit a ranch in New Mexico, they find the majority of their neighbours are hostile to strangers. Befriended by only one rancher, and plagued by rustlers, the thought of returning to England is tempting, but needing to prove himself, Rufus is coached as a fighter by a circus sharp shooter, the mysterious Ghost of the Cimarron. But will this be enough to overcome the frightening odds against him?

GAMBLER'S BULLETS

Robert Lane

The conquering of the American west threw up men with all the virtues and vices. The men of vision, ready to work hard to build a better life, were in the majority. But there were also work-shy gamblers, robbers and killers. Amongst these ne'er-do-wells were Melvyn Revett, Trevor Younis and Wilf Murray. But two determined men — Curtis Tyson and Neville Gough — took to the trail, and not until their last bullets were spent would they give up the fight against the lawless trio.

MIDNIGHT LYNCHING

Terry Murphy

When Ruby Malone's husband is lynched by a sheriff's posse, Wells Fargo investigator Asa Harker goes after the beautiful widow expecting her to lead him to the vast sum of money stolen from his company. But Ruby has gone on the outlaw trail with the handsome, young Ben Whitman. Worse still, Harker finds he must deal with a crooked sheriff. Without help, it looks as if he will not only fail to recover the stolen money but also lose his life into the bargain.

SMOKING STAR

B. J. Holmes

In the one-horse town of Medicine Bluff two men were dead. Sheriff Jack Starr didn't need the badge on his chest to spur him into tracking the killer. He had his own reason for seeking justice, a reason no-one knew. It drove him to take a journey into the past where he was to discover something else that was to add even greater urgency to the situation — to stop Montana's rivers running red with blood.

THE WIND WAGON

Troy Howard

Sheriff Al Corning was as tough as they came and with his four seasoned deputies he kept the peace in Laramie — at least until the squatters came. To fend off starvation, the settlers took some cattle off the cowmen, including Jonas Lefler. A hard, unforgiving man, Lefler retaliated with lynchings. Things got worse when one of the squatters revealed he was a fo___r Texas lawman — and no me___g ___ Could Sheriff Corning preve__ _ur-ther bloodshed?